TESTED

Book 4 of the Daniel Briggs Novels

C. G. COOPER

"TESTED"

A Corps Justice Daniel Briggs Novel
Copyright © 2017 C. G. Cooper. All Rights Reserved
Author: C. G. Cooper
Editors: Andrea Kerr & Cheryl Hopton

Dedications

In memory of Craig Crossman, a loyal member of Team

Cooper. We'll miss you, but hope you'll continue to sprinkle us with your blessings from Heaven. God Bless.

To my faithful readers: thank you for allowing me to continue this awesome writing journey. I could not do this without you.

- CGC

CHAPTER ONE

The first sip is my favorite. It always reminds me of the first kiss on a first date. It reminds me of one gentleman tipping his hat to another. It reminds me that there is an answer, and that answer can *always* be found at the bottom of the bottle, like a toy in a Cracker Jack box or a message in a fortune cookie.

I savored that first sip from the paper coffee cup. As I gazed over the vista of the Las Vegas strip from my cramped seat I saw only opportunity. I'd given up drinking, but somewhere between Seattle and San Francisco, a bottle of Jack Daniels had reappeared in my hand. I'd kicked the habit, and yet there was my old friend Jack, nestled in the crook of my arm. I'm sure if Jack could talk he'd say it was good to be back, and to have the buds reunited, hoping I would never again leave him behind. It was in those moments that I thought I could control him and the cravings. Like I said, everything seemed right with the world.

"Hey, Mister, can I have a drink?"

I turned to find a little boy sitting next to his sleeping mom. As far as I could remember, they'd boarded somewhere around Los Angeles. Up to this point he'd left me alone, talking with the rest of the passengers. They'd already been afforded the luxury of his eager questioning.

Now as he stared up at me, I wondered how a kid could be so uninhibited with strangers. His mom was lying next to him, and from her appearance, it looked like she'd worked every night shift since 1982.

"Sorry. It's just for adults," I said.

"Is it that stuff that burns? Mom said it burns a lot."

Did Mom have an alcohol problem, or had she kicked it like I had?

"Yeah, it burns," I said.

Not that I really wanted to dissuade the kid from having a future drink, but he was closer to five than fifteen. I felt it wise to be the good adult.

The kid stared at the bottle, looking like he was formulating another question. He wasn't put off by my demeanor. I didn't try to hide the fact that I wanted to be left alone. Except for the bus driver, I'd not said a word to anyone since Berkeley.

"We moved," the kid said quickly, like it was something he wasn't supposed to say.

"Did you live in Los Angeles?" I asked, surprising myself by extending the conversation.

"California," he corrected me.

"Right, California. Did you like California?"

He shrugged, again averting his eye. "Pete says it's always hot in Las Vegas. *Is* it always hot in Las Vegas?"

I wondered who Pete was.

"It depends on the time of year."

"Like because of the seasons?" he asked, brightening.

"Yeah, the seasons."

"Mom says we get to live in a hotel and that they're going to have donuts and waffles and granola bars."

He licked his lips, and I noticed his slightly hollow cheeks. After looking closer, I saw the dirt caked under his fingernails and his clothes appeared two sizes too small. Then I looked over at his mother, staring back at me, having roused from sleep. She did not regard me with hate or embarrassment, but rather with a look of resignation. The look reminded me of the look dogs have after suffering one too many beatings, before they give up the will to fight back.

"Nathaniel, leave the man alone," the mother said, her voice hoarse from sleep.

"But, Mom, I was just—"

"Nathaniel."

"It's okay, ma'am. He was just telling me about moving to Las Vegas. I'm the rude one. Nathaniel, my name is Daniel."

"Nathaniel and Daniel. That rhymes," the boy said, proud of himself for making the connection.

"Nathaniel, are you a betting man?" I asked.

"What's betting?" the boy asked.

"Let's say I ask you a question, and you get that question right. If you do, you win a prize."

"Wow, really? What kind of prize?"

"That's a surprise," I said.

"Prize and surprise. You rhymed again."

Nathaniel reminded me of a PFC in my last unit. He was from Chicago, and he would never shut up. Questions and rhymes, always the rhymes, although his rhymes were of the vulgar pedigree. I couldn't remember his name now, and the last time I'd seen him both of his legs had been blown off. I shoved that memory away and refocused on Nathaniel.

"So, Nathaniel, are you a betting man?"

The boy nodded eagerly.

"Okay," I said. "What state is Las Vegas in?"

Nathaniel scrunched his eyes shut, thinking hard. His palms tapped on his thighs until he sprang up out of his seat, his mouth bursting open, and said, "Nevada! Las Vegas is in Nevada!"

"That's right. You win the prize."

"Mom. Mom, Daniel says I win a prize. What is it?"

I turned toward the window so he couldn't see what I was doing. I pulled out my wallet and slid out a couple bills. I wrapped the larger one in a one-dollar bill and then handed it to Nathaniel. "It's all yours, kid, but why don't you let your mom hold on to it for safekeeping?"

The boy held it up like he had won an Olympic medal. Then, dutifully, he handed it to his mother, and I wondered if that was a routine. He had done it so naturally. Usually kids don't like to give up their prizes.

I watched the mother give Nathaniel a tired smile, and then she took the money. She unwrapped the bills to prep them for insertion into her voluminous purse when her eyes went wide. She'd found the one hundred-dollar bill. I put my finger to my lips when she looked at me. Nathaniel didn't need to know. She mouthed a silent "thank you." There were no tears in her eyes. Maybe she was used to getting handouts, but I saw real gratitude there. For some unknown reason, I knew that unless that money was pried from her hands, she would use it to take care of her boy.

She tucked the bills into a secret corner of her purse, nodded at me once, and then closed her eyes.

———

I HADN'T BEEN to Las Vegas in years, not since the crazy weekend after we completed training at Twentynine Palms. The years might have improved the landscape, now filled with new hotels, shinier cars, and more gamblers, but to me it all felt the same. The dry air, mixed with the enticing pull of possibility, greeted me as I stepped off the bus. Nathaniel and his mother followed a few moments later.

The boy tugged on my sleeve. "Hey, Daniel, do you want to come visit us?"

His mother didn't seem to notice. She was scanning the loitering crowd at the bus station looking for something or someone.

"Maybe I'll see you around. You save some of those waffles for me, okay?"

"You like strawberries or just syrup?"

I couldn't help but smile. "Both."

"Okay, strawberries and syrup. I'll save you some."

I stuck out my hand. He took in his little hand like we had just closed a multimillion-dollar deal.

"You take care of yourself, Nathaniel."

"I will."

Then they were off with Nathaniel being dragged along by his still-searching mother. He waved at me, and I waved back, and then went in search of a vending machine. The booze was getting to me now.

Lightweight, I thought, bouncing my paper cup into a trash can. Then for some reason I took my bag off my shoulder, unzipped it, and extracted the bottle of Jack Daniels. If Jack had a face, he would have been smiling at me at that moment saying, "Come on, buddy. Let's go have some fun." It was the old battle waging inside me, igniting like a stick of dynamite.

Where had I gone wrong? I *had* kicked the habit. Now here it was again. My vigilance had been lulled into complacency. And my old friend slipped in—my partner in crime. I thought of all that had happened over the previous months and all the progress that I had made, and it made me feel ashamed. I had never been to treatment or a single AA meeting. I didn't need that. At least that's what I told myself. I had been through the hardships of war and had come out the other side unscathed. Again, that was another little lie I liked to tell myself. Unscathed in the physical sense maybe, but there was more than one way to be damaged or injured.

I closed my eyes and pushed away the urge to put good old Jack back in my bag. Instead, I gave my old friend a respectful nod and tossed him in the trash.

Freed from that burden for the time being, I resumed my search for a vending machine. With the alcohol gone, I had a sudden craving for a candy bar. A Baby Ruth was my favorite, but a Snickers would do in a pinch. I never found the vending machine.

Instead I found Nathaniel and his mother. She was speaking to two men. I might have been oblivious to the tension if I hadn't noticed her shielding Nathaniel behind her. She had him pinned in place with both of her hands. I moved closer to better hear what was being said.

The first words from the men assaulted my ears.

"We didn't say nothing 'bout no boy."

"But I couldn't leave him."

"I don't give a shit what you do with him. The deal struck was for only you."

"He won't be any trouble, I promise. He's a good boy."

The man was looking around now as if he sensed an enemy's presence. Then he refocused on Nathaniel's mother. Anger turned his huge head and meaty forearms a dark red.

"Now, you listen here, bitch—"

"Hey, Nathaniel," I interrupted.

Nathaniel and the two men turned to face me, but Nathaniel's mother's eyes remained locked on Meaty Forearms.

"Hey," Nathaniel said, his earlier exuberance having evaporated.

"I was going to take one of those sightseeing tours of the

city, and I wondered if you and your mom wanted to tag along."

"Wow. Hey, mom, can we? Can we?"

His mother didn't say a word.

Meaty Forearms glared at me. "Move along, asshole."

The Beast inside of me began to stir, stretching its muscled body, easing to its feet. I had been called an asshole a thousand times before, so the word didn't bother me. Rather, it was the reaction it had elicited from Nathaniel. It had been like watching a light doused and his spirit broken that evoked the vengeance I now sought. His countenance echoed his mother's facial expressions.

Meaty Forearms stepped around mother and son. He pointed his grimy finger in my face, but I didn't move. Inside me, The Beast was spinning circles like a caged animal; it begged to be let out. Meaty Forearm's finger stabbed at my chest. I knew he was going to say something like, "You have no idea who you're dealing with," or "You'd better get out of here before I kick your ass."

It was only natural because he was protecting his turf. He was used to being the man in charge. Well, he and his trusty sidekick, Crazy Hair, that is. But they'd never met *me* before. Before the words could leave his mouth, his thick finger was trapped in my vice-like grip. He found himself on his knees in less than a second, looking up at me with a look of pain in his bulging eyes.

"Say you're sorry," I said calmly.

"What?" he asked stupidly.

My hand flexed, and his finger snapped with a sickening crunch.

"Sorry. I'm sorry."

"Don't say it to me. Tell Nathaniel and his mother."

The Beast was calling to me now, begging me to lash out, pummel the man, put him in his place. *Not yet*, I assured it.

"I'm sorry, okay? I'm sorry."

I let go of his finger, and the man cradled his damaged appendage. He stood on shaky legs and glanced over at Crazy Hair.

That was all it took. Crazy Hair's hands were already balled up, ready for the fight. He rushed at me with five long strides. To me, it felt like a mile. He broadcast every move with the staggering hitch in his step. He overcompensated with his other leg. He was a bigger man, accustomed to using his size to take down his opponents. It was apparent that at least one of his opponents had gotten the best of him. He had one bum leg.

Should I make it two?, I thought, as I stepped to the side at the last possible moment, and delivered a solid, yet not quite crushing, blow to his handicapped knee. *Na. One will do.* As the pain exploded in his knee, he toppled to the ground like I'd just chopped down a tree. *Timber.*

Meaty Forearms looked like he wanted to rejoin the fight. When he looked at me, I shot him a glare that negated any action and cut off any further remarks. Whether it was the steely look I had given him or the crowd that had started to gather, he thought better of his chances. Instead, he chose to help his hobbled friend, and they left in a battered pickup truck.

Once they were gone, Nathaniel resumed his bubbly personality again. "Wow, Mom. Did you see that? Daniel's like a superhero."

Even my actions didn't make Nathaniel's mother smile. She had been through similar confrontations before, and she knew the future inevitably had more in store.

"I was going to catch a cab into town. You guys want to come along? It's my treat," I said. Nathaniel looked at his mother, who nodded.

Only after the cab pulled away from the bus station did I

realize Nathaniel's mom had lost her deal. She was staring out the window with vacant eyes. Whatever arrangements she had made before venturing to Las Vegas had vanished because of my actions.

I had come to Las Vegas for a fresh start. Sure, there had been a little hiccup along the way with old buddy Jack trying to nudge his way back into my life, but I still was on a fresh start. Why Vegas? Call it the warped mind of a Marine, a grunt who gets a strange kick out of volunteering for the toughest things.

I'd looked at a map of the United States, and there it was, a siren calling to me with neon accents: Sin City. A bastion of sin and greed to many, but to me it represented opportunity. I had no idea what that opportunity was other than a challenge - something I relished.

I wanted a fresh start and a place where no one knew my past. Part of me wanted to dump Nathaniel and his mother at the next stop. Maybe I'd give them another hundred bucks and wish them well. I had my fresh start to protect. That didn't include looking after some kid or his mother who looked like a washed-up diner waitress.

I watched Nathaniel try to get a better view of the city by bouncing in his seat. I knew I couldn't just leave them. I had been the protector, and as much as I tried to run from that, I always got sucked back into that vortex. It was as if the universe was saying, "Daniel Briggs, I know what you *want* to be, but this is what you *will* be." Thus, I went along with the universe's plans. Little did I know that staying with Nathaniel and his mom would lead me on the most dangerous path of my life.

CHAPTER TWO

"Were those friends of yours?" I asked, trying to remember Nathaniel's mother's name. I realized I hadn't asked her name yet.

"I was supposed to be working for them," she said. "But now—"

"I'm sorry if I screwed things up for you, but I'm not sorry that I stepped in."

She shook her head like it didn't matter. "It's probably for the best. A friend back in L.A. hooked me up with them, but you're probably right. I guess I should have been upfront about Nathaniel. Besides, I could smell the booze all over them."

"What's booze, Mommy?"

"Don't worry about it, honey. I'll find another job, and we'll be just fine. What do you say we go get some ice cream when we get there?"

"Where are we going? Can I have chocolate with sprinkles?" Nathaniel asked.

"Sure," she said.

The taxi driver decided to butt into the conversation.

"Hey, if you're looking for a job, my sister's a maid over at The Mirage. She said they're looking for more girls. The pay's not super great, but at least it's a start. Ask for Sheila, and tell her Bernard sent you."

There didn't seem to be any ill intention in Bernard's voice so I kept my mouth shut. Or maybe I just kept my mouth shut because otherwise Nathaniel's mother might smell the booze on *my* breath. *Had Nathaniel's father been a drunk?*

The taxi rolled along with the two adults in the back seat contemplating their next moves.

———

WE SETTLED into a beat-up motel on a dingy street in a seedy part of town. Even if you stood on the motel's roof, you most likely couldn't see the lights of Vegas. Its paint was a pale pink, but it could have been a bright neon at some point. The motel looked as worn as Nathaniel's mother.

I requested two rooms, paying with cash. The cashier barely looked up. She provided my change before stuffing her hand back into an industrial-sized Cheetos bag.

"Two eleven and two twelve," she said as a Cheeto flew from her mouth. "No loud music after ten, and keep visitors to a minimum."

"Got it. Thanks," I said, snatching the two room keys.

"Do I get to stay with Daniel?" Nathaniel asked.

"You don't want to sleep with me, buddy; I snore," the little white lie came to my lips without thinking. Why had I lied? I don't snore. I was quite possibly the quietest sleeper known to man. It was a good talent to have if you were a Marine sniper.

"What about ice cream? Will you come get ice cream with us?"

"How about a rain check? I've got a few things to take care of, but I'll see you later tonight. Okay?"

Nathaniel looked disappointed, but he didn't complain out loud. *Good kid.*

"I'll pay you back for the room and for the other thing," his mother blurted out. "I'll check out that job at the Mirage, and I promise I'll get you the money."

"You can pay me back for the room, but not for the other thing," I said, winking at Nathaniel.

We went our separate ways. Part of me thought that maybe I should just leave and find another place to stay; they would never find me. I could be just another anonymous face on the bustling streets of Las Vegas.

But I couldn't do that to Nathaniel or to his mother. Maybe this was why I'd come here—to help them in some way. I already had, but, well, it wasn't like I actually had any firm plans. I never did anymore. The plan had been to get to Las Vegas, and here I was. Rather than going to my room, I pocketed the key, opting to go for a walk. In part this had become a habit, but I also didn't want to sit down. I needed to keep moving so I could think.

Before long I found myself standing in front of a building that could be the sister of the motel where I was staying. Its sad façade sagged in the sunlight as if years of exposure had melted it like candle wax. The bar was open despite the early hour. I reminded myself that this was Vegas and nothing closed. Want to play a card game at seven in the morning? Not a problem. Need a martini at nine? No problem. That was Vegas.

Not knowing what the establishment would hold, I stepped out of the sunlight into the dark bar. The smell of decades' worth of cigarettes smoked and barrels of beer spilled greeted me. The assault on my senses was like an old drunk uncle - familiar, yet repulsive at the same time.

A woman behind the bar looked up when I walked in. She then resumed wiping out an oversized beer mug with a dirty dishtowel. I made a mental note not to order a beer.

I sat down at the only table that didn't have chairs stacked on top of it. Apparently, management *did* mop the floors every day. It had that going for it.

I didn't know what I was doing there. Testing myself, maybe? Daring my willpower to cave? The bartender was in her fifties, and she wore a pink top at least four sizes too small, causing her boobs to almost tumble out. She sauntered over and asked what I wanted; I ordered an orange juice.

She cocked her head to one side and said, "You want to make that a double?" sarcasm thick in her voice.

"Just the one, please. No ice."

When she returned, I slipped her a ten-dollar bill across the table.

"You want change?" she asked.

"No. You keep it," I said. The juice probably cost two bucks. In fact, she probably hadn't even rung it up yet. It was ten dollars in her pocket. She gave me a brilliant smile as if she had just registered my arrival.

"If you need anything at all, I'll be right over there."

"Thanks," I said, sipping the orange juice. It was too sweet for my taste buds, but I didn't complain.

There I sat while minutes ticked by, as the orange juice drained, sip by sip. It was like an hourglass draining away sand, slipping down to nothing except the loss of my resolve, maybe. I'd taken to measuring how far down the juice would go with each sip. I estimated I had another four sips to go until I was finished.

As I began to take the first of the remaining four sips, the door to the bar slammed open. Brilliant sunlight spilled into the dank room, pouring men half wrestling into the establishment. At first I thought it was a fight, and my body tensed.

Then I recognized the sound of laughter. Someone said, "Don't grab my ass, man."

"Hey, Lurlene," the tallest one said. He was probably a little bit taller than me with the physique of a college high jumper. The second man was the shortest of the three, and I immediately noticed that he was missing an ear. The third man was as nondescript as a grain of sand on a community beach. I pegged them immediately. The tall one was the leader, the second man was the number two, with Mr. Nondescript as the tagalong.

"Hey, boys! You want the usual?" the bartender asked, but the smile she gave them was not quite as brilliant as the one she had given me.

"Yes, ma'am. Three of the same, please."

They walked to the table closest to the bar. They removed the chairs and set them upright on the floor as if this they had done a thousand times before.

"What'd you get today?" Lurlene asked, while handing out the three overflowing mugs of beer.

"Only two. We could have had more, but Benji shot high, scared the rest away."

"I thought you guys said *on* three, not *after* three," Benji, the tag along, protested.

"Wait. You *can* count to three?" asked Mr. No Ear.

"Shut up, Jay."

,

Lurlene laughed like she'd heard it all before.

"You three still getting paid to do that?" she asked.

"You think I'd be hanging out with these two knuckleheads if I wasn't?" Mr. High Jumper answered with a grin.

"You just tell me when you're taking on customers again. You know I don't mind getting paid," Lurlene said, slapping Mr. High Jumper on the arm playfully. She returned to the bar.

"I will pay you a handsome referral fee for every customer you bring our way," High Jumper said, like he was doling out stock options on Wall Street.

Lurlene slid behind the bar. Then to my surprise she pointed straight at me, "Well, how about him? Maybe he wants to go."

All eyes turned in my direction. I should have finished my orange juice and left, but something held me in place.

"What do you say, Mister? Wanna do some coyote hunting?" Benji asked.

"Is it legal?" I asked.

"Yes, it's legal," High Jumper said, "Who do you think we are, riffraff?

Lurlene giggled, and Jay, the earless one, laughed.

"Seriously, coyotes are a real problem. They eat people's dogs and small livestock. Landowners pay us by the head. It's only a small fee if you'd like to join. We'll give you ten percent of each one you kill. It is possible to make your money back in one night – if you're a good shot," High Jumper winked at me.

It was an easy no. They must be running a scam. Maybe there were no coyotes, and I was paying for a one-way trip into the desert. *I should have said no.*

For some reason that I couldn't explain at the time, my lips moved and the words that came out were, "Sure, I'll go."

CHAPTER THREE

To this day, I don't know why I agreed.

You could say that I was up for adventure. It'd been a long time since I had thrown caution to the wind.

One might argue I wanted to try something new because, on some primal level, I felt bored with my life.

Looking back now, I could see the universe was pushing me in whichever direction it needed me to go. As I sat in that bar, I believed it was my choice. When the three men joined me at my table, I welcomed them without my typical hesitancy. It's not that I'm a social outcast or incapable of holding conversations. Rather, in my line of work, it is easier for me to keep people at arm's length, or just avoid getting involved at all.

Mr. High Jumper's name was Tom. He was a natural storyteller. Upon wrapping up his tale, I could imagine millions of coyotes descending like locusts upon Las Vegas. That wasn't the case, of course, but a good storyteller can make you think and feel certain ways, depending on his stories. With Tom's sidekicks staring at me with anticipation, I found it easy to get caught up in the excitement.

"So, what do you say about spending some time on the dusty trails, just the four of us?" Tom asked.

I thought of Nathaniel and his mother, even though they weren't really my responsibility. But as often was the case, I had made them my concern. I was pulled in by the animated looks dancing on the three men's faces staring at me from across the table.

"You never told me the amount of the fee," I said.

"First, have you fired a weapon before?" Tom asked.

"A few times."

"Okay, you get a discount for that. Second, what about rifles? Have you ever shot a rifle?"

"A bit."

Tom didn't need to look to his friends for approval of the new member; he was their ringleader. The funny thing was, although he was putting on a show for my benefit, never once did he remind me of a hustler. I got the feeling these men held no false pretenses; they truly enjoyed coyote hunting. It provided an outlet for three men who probably held blue-collar jobs. They enjoyed spending their days off kicking up dust in the wilds outside of Las Vegas.

"You look like a pretty straight up guy," Tom said. "How does $250 sound?"

I thought about it for a moment before I countered, "I'll go with $250 providing you give me twenty percent of the bounty rather than ten percent."

Tom sat back in his chair, crossing his arms over his chest. "Well, I'm not sure about that; we're kind of sticklers for the ten percent rule. It's worked out well for us this far."

I leaned closer, putting my elbows on the table. "And I'll bet most people you take out there don't shoot many coyotes. Let me put it this way: I get twenty percent, and I'll find myself some coyotes. Soon your eighty percent will begin to feel like one hundred percent."

Benji fidgeted, and Jay was looking back and forth between Tom and me. Tom just stared at me, and then in the blink of an eye, he smiled and stuck out his hand. "You've got yourself a deal."

I received directions about where to meet them on the back of my crinkled bar receipt. After finishing my orange juice, I bid them farewell. As I stepped outside, the sun was slipping beyond the horizon. A prostitute in hot pink tights walked by and gave me a wink. *Sorry lady. You're not my type.* But even the grunge of the inhabitants and the trash on the streets couldn't dampen my spirits. The thought of leaving the city to spend time with people my own age was exciting. The cherry on top was holding and firing a weapon again. It felt right.

I'd never minded being on patrol. As long as I was on point, I was happy. My fellow Marines called it "the sixth sense." I just thought of it as being aware of my surroundings. "Situational awareness" was the official term provided in the Marine Corps. Although I had never thought of myself as "special," proof to the contrary was that I'd never once been shot or blown up. *Or was that just dumb luck?*

As I walked back to the motel, I thought about the supplies I might need on this trip. Tom had suggested bringing a few snacks, some water, and the fee, of course. They would take care of the rest. I knew I couldn't buy a weapon on such short notice. Besides, even if I could buy a rifle, I had no place to hide it. I'd just have to use whatever they had. *No big deal.*

When I arrived at the motel, Nathaniel and his mother were just returning. The little boy waved to me. Once they'd crossed the street, he ran up to me to say hello.

"Hey, Daniel, guess what?"

"Hmm, let's see. Did you get your ice cream?"

"No, not yet. This is even better."

"Hmm, you met a clown, and he let you swing on a trapeze?"

"No, silly. I don't like clowns."

"Okay, then I give up," I said.

"Mom got a job. Isn't that awesome?"

"That's great, Buddy. Congratulations to both of you."

The news didn't seem to excite the mom as much. I sensed this job was another in a long list of small-time gigs. Maybe it was eclipsed only by a longer list of disappointments. Had it always been that way, or had she dropped out of high school or college when she'd had Nathaniel? It was tough to determine her age. She wore no makeup, and her face spoke of a hard life. She could've been twenty-one or forty-three.

"Nathaniel, I was wondering if you could help me out with something."

"Sure!" the boy said without hesitation.

"I've been kind of rude to someone, and I'm not sure how to make things right."

"Mom says when you're rude, you should say you're sorry. Maybe shake their hand or something."

"Okay. That's a good idea, but here's the problem. What if you don't know the person's name? What are you supposed to do then?"

"You don't even know the person's name?"

I shrugged like I was the dumbest person in the world. Nathaniel laughed at me and then huffed in exasperation. "You should just ask them their name."

That's exactly what I did. I turned to his mother and said, "Nathaniel's mom, I'm sorry I never asked for your name. I'm Daniel Briggs." I stuck out my hand, and she took it. It was the first smile she had given me since meeting her. She was shy; I could see that now.

"Veronica," she said quietly, "Veronica Taylor."

"Yeah, that's our last name," Nathaniel said. "We used to have a different last name, but Mom likes the name Taylor better."

Veronica quickly withdrew her hand.

"It's a pleasure to meet you, Veronica. Now, I don't know about you two, but I'm starving. How about we get a bite to eat?"

"Hey, Mom. Can we go? Can we?"

"Of course," Veronica said.

"What about ice cream? Can we *finally* have some ice cream?"

"Sure." Veronica smiled at her son and then looked up at me. For a second I saw a glint of humanity. Call it hope, or the fact that the day had turned out pretty good. Either way, I now realized that she was younger than I had previously thought. She might be in her early twenties, and I'm not sure why that should have surprised me. It might've been because she was on the road as a single mom.

Something about the contrast of Nathaniel's exuberance with Veronica's cold acceptance of life piqued my interest. I wanted to find out her entire story, and unbeknownst to me, I would find out that and much more.

CHAPTER FOUR

Veronica and I spent most of dinner listening to Nathaniel explain the trip to his mom's job interview. He described leaping roller coasters at New York-New York, the castle towers at Excalibur, and the lion head of the MGM Grand.

"There were people everywhere, Daniel. Some were dressed up. Some had kids. It really looked like everybody was having loads of fun. I asked Mom if we could go do what the other people were doing. She said maybe later. You want to come with us?"

"I'd like that," I said, again surprising myself.

"When we got to the hotel that Mom's gonna work at, they took us to the back where the performers rehearse." He covered his mouth and giggled. "There were ladies in their underwear. Then there were guys doing somersaults and stuff. Mom said they put on shows, and those people were getting ready."

He went on to describe the people he had met and related conversations he had during his mom's interview. The way he retold it you would have thought he had been there for days. His level of enthusiasm was infectious, and I smiled as he described the man dressed up as a woman. Then he told of the women with painted faces that looked like dragons.

I was so caught up in Nathaniel's story that I barely watched Veronica. Her dinner plate was still full when dessert arrived.

"Not hungry?" I asked.

She shook her head, but nibbled on a French fry.

"Mom doesn't eat much," Nathaniel said. "If I don't like what I'm eating, she lets me eat her food."

As if to make the point, he reached over and grabbed a pile of fries from her plate. Veronica didn't say a word. If it had been any other kid, I would have considered him a spoiled brat. But the way in which he did this let me know it was a routine for them. I got the feeling as I learned more about them, she'd given up a lot to care for Nathaniel. It wasn't the time to ask what had happened. That type of conversation could wait until he was in bed.

"You know, on the way over here I realized I forgot to ask you a very important question," I said.

"What?" Nathaniel asked, with a mouthful of fries.

"I forgot to ask you what grade you're in."

The boy's chest puffed out, and he said, "I'm in the first grade."

"I'll bet you're one of the smartest kids in your class, aren't you?" Nathaniel nodded. "Are you done for the school year, or are you going to start up school here?"

Nathaniel looked at his mother, who nodded with obvious discomfort.

"We were going to figure that out when we got here," she said, stuffing a French fry in her mouth.

"I'm going to miss my teacher," Nathaniel explained, "but Mom said there are good teachers here, too. Is that true?"

"It is," I said. "I'm sure they'll stick you with the best teacher they've got."

I don't know why I stretched the truth for him. It might have been because Veronica looked ready to run. More important, I wanted to pretend for him everything would be okay. What could you say to a kid who had been dragged on the road, taken away from his school *and* his home?

"What about you, Daniel? What are you going to do here?" Nathaniel asked.

"That's a very good question. I'll probably start looking for a job. Your mom's lucky; she's already got one. In the next few days, I need to figure out what I want to do."

"Well, what are you good at?" Nathaniel asked, wiping his mouth on the back of his sleeve.

"I guess you could say I'm good at a little bit of everything."

"Well, what do you *like* to do?"

That's when the pang hit me. Nathaniel's question sparked such an intense urge to have a drink that I actually winced. Luckily, neither of them noticed.

"I don't know what I like to do. That's why I came here, and there's a lot to choose from."

Nathaniel answered with a grave nod, as if he'd been thinking the same thing.

———

I said goodnight to Nathaniel. He gave me a high five before slipping into the room for some well-earned television time before his bedtime.

Veronica closed the door behind him. "Thanks for dinner," she said. "I guess I should pay you back for that, too."

"Don't worry about it," I said. "It's just nice to have

company. Having you and Nathaniel along is kind of a treat for me." She nodded distractedly. "So, when do you start work?" I asked, uncomfortable with the silence.

"Tomorrow," she said, pausing awkwardly. "I was wondering if—I know I just met you—or *we* just met you, but I was wondering if you could watch Nathaniel for me. They want me to start training at 10 am, and I should be back before 5 pm."

I would meet Tom and his buddies the next day, but not until 6 pm, so I said, "Sure. I'll take him for a tour around town. Would that be okay?"

"He'd like that," Veronica said. "Thanks. I really appreciate it. We haven't had much luck with people lately. It's nice to meet someone like you. You know, somebody good."

That was the moment I should have told her that I *was not* a good person. I'd seen and done awful things. If she knew the truth, she wouldn't want me even in the same city as her son much less alone with him.

For some reason, I didn't say a thing. I kept my stupid mouth shut about my past. Instead said, "I'll come by at 9:30 am."

Veronica nodded and went into the hotel room. I waited by the door until I heard both the deadbolt click and the chain slip into place.

I wasn't tired, so I went for a walk. This was a new habit to avoid drinking. I started with a loop around the motel. Then I began walking larger concentric circles into the surrounding neighborhood.

Two hours passed before I returned. During that time, although the itch wanted scratching, I didn't stop at a single bar—another minor victory.

After I took one more loop around the motel, I'd be ready for bed.

I was fifty feet from their vehicle when I saw Meaty Forearms and Shaky Leg from the bus station.

I got lucky because I came in at just the right angle. The guys in the white Cadillac couldn't see me, but I saw their silhouettes. They were staring in the opposite direction. When I followed their gaze, I thought it was just coincidence, but it wasn't. I took my steps with caution to remain out of sight, in case one should look in either the rear-view or the side mirrors.

In the next thirty seconds, two things happened. First, the light in Veronica and Nathaniel's room went out. Second, my *buddies* from the bus station got out of the car and sauntered towards the motel. It was obvious they hadn't gotten the hint.

I did the natural thing; I went to have a talk with them.

CHAPTER FIVE

I was following Meaty Forearms and Shaky Leg at a discrete distance. They were so focused on their destination that they weren't aware of my presence. The Beast inside me growled, desiring action. I decided to err on the side of caution because of the potential witnesses going about their nightly routines. Casual handclasps resulted in the exchange of drugs. Provocatively dressed women were trying to sell their night's first tricks as they whispered in the ears of interested men.

Targets one and two hit the upper walkway. It was time to make my move. I couldn't let them reach the door. I couldn't let Nathaniel see what I was about to do. The Beast stretched its legs and waited, so I bounded up the stairs to my quarry. I let out a low whistle, and the men turned to face me.

Meaty Forearms had his finger in one of those metal splints, and Shaky Leg was balanced uncomfortably on his damaged leg. Both wore light windbreakers which was a hint that they might be armed. Maybe they weren't completely stupid. Guns wouldn't do them any good in public. They must have known that because they didn't reach for their waistbands. Instead they made a show of putting their hands to their sides.

Meaty Forearms again assumed the role of spokesman, "There are ten more guys on their way," he said.

"I don't believe you. Remember, I told you to leave us alone."

They did not take a step closer. They were two against one. Maybe they *had* learned their lesson at the bus stop. Nobody wants more than one broken finger in a day.

"Look, we're just doing our jobs, okay?" Shaky Leg said, his anxiety obvious. Meaty Forearms actually elbowed him in the abdomen. It was like watching a scene from a black and white rerun from *The Three Stooges*, the exception was they lacked the third Stooge.

"Is it your job to harass young mothers? They wouldn't give you a job working at the grocery store, huh?"

"No! It's nothing like that, okay? Look, she signed a contract. I've got a copy right here. Would you like to see it?" Shaky Leg asked.

"Consider the contract cancelled," I said. "If she can't take the kid, she's not going."

"Look, I'm sorry if things got out of hand at the bus station. We had kind of a long night, and we weren't even supposed to be the ones to pick her up. Things got a little heated. It's not the way we usually work. I promise."

Why was Shaky Leg taking the lead on this? I had thought Meaty Forearms was the leader of the pair, but it turned out he was just the muscle. Shaky Leg was the brains of the operation.

"She signed up to work at a place that's not good for kids. I knew that, but she signed the contract. Our boss won't let it drop until we bring her in—without her kid. "

"Ball up the contract, and throw it to me," I said.

Shaky Leg did as I ordered. I snatched the paper ball out of the air, careful to keep an eye on them. Upon scanning the contract, I noticed there was no letterhead. It was direct and to the point. In one page, it detailed her position as a *hostess*, stating her base pay plus tips. Employment afforded her a two-day on, one-day off schedule.

There was a single bold line on the contract that specified, "No family allowed". The definition of family was spelled out as including boyfriends, kids, and even pets. It wasn't until I reached the bottom that I knew the name of the employer. Below the manager's signature was the name of the employer, The Frisky Filly. Veronica had signed a contract to work as a prostitute.

I crumpled the contract back up and threw it at Shaky Leg. He ignored it like many more copies of the contract existed.

"Tell your boss I want to buy out her contract."

"Won't go for that," Shaky Leg said.

"I don't care what you think. Tell him I'm doing it. Within two days of him providing me a fair price, I will pay it in full."

Now Meaty Forearms stepped forward. "You don't have that kind of money. You know how much money we make off these girls?"

"I can only imagine," I said.

"I mean, look at you. When's the last time you took a shower or shaved? Your clothes look like something Mommy saved for you from the 90s."

"Shut up, Wayne," Shaky Leg said.

To me, he said, "I'll talk to the boss, but I know he won't be happy."

"Tell him there's plenty of girls out there he can get his filthy hands on. This one's not for sale."

Shaky Leg nodded and grabbed Meaty Forearms's arm. They took the long way across the catwalk instead of asking for permission to return the way they'd arrived. *Smart move.* Now I had to talk to Veronica to find out why she'd made the decision to become a *hostess* in Las Vegas, and why had she brought Nathaniel along for the twisted ride?

CHAPTER SIX

Something was off. I know mothers will do most anything to protect their children. While I didn't think that Veronica was abusing Nathaniel, there was always the possibility of other nefarious things occurring behind the scenes. I'd seen too many seemingly normal human beings act in ways that were both outrageous and inhumane. Still, I couldn't believe a woman suckered into a contract with a place like The Frisky Filly would neglect the proper care of her child.

When I stepped in front of the door to Room 211, I was fully prepared to be the interrogator. I knocked softly, in case Nathaniel was asleep. When Veronica answered the door, she put her finger to her lips and pointed back into the room.

"I was about to go to sleep," she whispered.

"Sorry, but this can't wait."

Her eyes searched mine. I wasn't going to back down.

"Okay, let me grab a sweater." She shivered and was gone for a moment. She returned wrapped in a threadbare sweater that would do little to ward off the slightest of breezes. She flipped the top door lock and stepped outside. Then she just stood there, arms hugging her body, waiting for me to start. It was still warm outside but she acted like she was freezing.

"Our friends from the bus station paid us a visit." She didn't seem surprised. "They showed me your contract." Veronica still did not register a reaction. "Did Nathaniel know what you were going to be doing here in Vegas?"

"Of course not."

"When were you going to tell him?"

"I wasn't going to tell him. I was going to get a sitter during the times I was working. Actually, I had a sitter lined up, but she fell through. Those guys weren't supposed to ever see Nathaniel."

"But you told them you were coming. I saw you looking for them at the bus stop."

Veronica exhaled. "Actually, I was looking for my friend. She's the one that helped me get the job. She works at The Frisky Filly, and she called me one day saying they were looking for more girls. I asked how much they were paying. I had to go to the UPS Store to sign and fax the contract back, but I'd never seen those guys before. I've only talked to the manager over the phone."

"Do you think your friend told them what time you were arriving?"

Veronica just shrugged. Her apathy was really starting to bother me. *Screw up your own life in any way you choose, just don't bring a little kid into your sordid mess*, I thought, but I never spoke the words.

"I guess I should go talk to them," she said finally. "See if I can set things right."

"I told them I'd buy out your contract," I said.

Her eyes blazed. "You didn't have to do that. You don't even know me."

"I don't have to know you. I saw that you're in trouble, and I just wanted to—"

"We are *not* your responsibility. Look, I should have the money in a couple days. I'll pay you back for the hotel room. I think it's best if you just find somewhere else to stay and don't come around again."

"What about tomorrow? Who's going to watch Nathaniel for you?"

She'd forgotten about that.

"I'll figure something out. I can take him with me. Someone said they might have a nursery at the hotel. Like I said, *we're* not your responsibility."

I didn't want to push her off the edge. This was the most emotion she'd shown in the short time that I'd known her. She was angry at me, but it was good to see a little fire from the tired woman.

"Look, I'm not doing anything tomorrow. I'll look after Nathaniel for you. You go to work, and then we'll figure things out."

It took her almost a minute to make her decision. The exhausted look returned to her features and she nodded.

"Fine. But after tomorrow—"

"I know, I'll leave you both alone."

With that, she turned and stepped back into the motel room. Before the door closed, I saw something odd. Her ponytail was slightly askew, like it'd been nudged out of place. Stranger still was the bald head I could see from underneath the wig.

The door closed softly. I left, wondering why Veronica wore a wig.

CHAPTER SEVEN

I t wasn't my first sleepless night, and I was sure it
wouldn't be my last. Veronica's contract wasn't an issue
for me because I had the money. What preoccupied my
thoughts as I sat in my darkened room, peering through the
blinds, was the low probability my offer would be accepted.
Although I didn't have unlimited funds, I had enough. I had
access to more, if needed, but I hoped it wouldn't come down
to that.

The problem, as I saw it, was if The Frisky Filly's management didn't want to negotiate, they might insist Veronica
fulfill the terms of her contract. Where did that leave her? I
had met girls who'd made similar deals. I'd known American
strippers in Guam, as well as prostitutes in Jacksonville,
North Carolina. When you first met them, they'd act proud
of their situation. They would often brag about how much
money they made and how well management took care of
them. After a while, you learned they'd gotten themselves
into situations they were unable to escape.

While I scanned the parking lot, that was what kept my
mind churning into the early morning hours. I'd never needed

much sleep. From experience, I knew I could go two nights without rest.

My brain clicked back to a more urgent topic. Why was Veronica wearing a wig? It was possible it was just her thing. Maybe she'd gone through a rebellious phase, and she had shaved off all her hair. Or maybe she kept it that way, wearing her fake hair whenever she chose. Anything was possible, I guess. In my opinion, the most obvious answer was probably the right one. It could explain so many things, like her resignation, lack of warmth, and her bedraggled appearance.

She was sick.

By the time the sun rose, I had showered and dressed in the only extra set of clothes I had. I was ready to put my game plan into effect. Nine o'clock rolled around, and I went next door. Veronica answered the door looking like she'd stayed up all night too. She let me inside and starting peppering me with the rules.

"Don't let him eat junk food all day," Veronica instructed me. "He should probably get some rest around one."

"Oh, come on, Mom. I don't want to take a nap."

"I didn't say a nap, honey; I said rest. It's going to be hot out today, and I don't want you to wear yourself out."

"Don't worry, we'll take it easy," I said.

There was no nod of thanks as she left. She didn't even give me a twenty-dollar bill to make sure Nathaniel was fed. She just left with weary steps, like a prisoner being sent to the gallows.

Nathaniel was dressed and ready to go, but I really wanted to stay in the motel. I needed to see if any uninvited guests came by, but I could tell by the look on Nathaniel's face, that wasn't going to happen. Instead of suggesting we settle in and watch some television, I said "How about we grab some breakfast? I'd do anything for some French toast right now."

"What's French toast?"

"You've never had French toast?" I asked.

"I like pancakes and eggs and bacon."

"Well let me tell you, if we can find a place that makes some decent French toast, you may never eat pancakes again."

Nathaniel rolled his eyes the way kids do, like I'd just said that Earth was made of Jell-O.

"How about if you get pancakes, and I'll let you try a bite of my French toast?"

"Okay," Nathaniel said, sticking out his hand. We shook on it. Again, he took on the role of a cultured businessman.

He ate all his pancakes, half my French toast, a double helping of scrambled eggs and a crispy pile of bacon. It was an impressive breakfast for a kid of Nathaniel's stature. When he was done, he sat back in his chair, closed his eyes, and rubbed his belly.

"Are you ready for your nap?" I asked.

His eyes popped wide open. "You're not going to make me take a nap, are you? I'm not three."

"Okay, okay. As long as you promise to drink some water today, I won't make you take a nap."

He nodded self-assuredly, like he'd won a well-fought chess match. With Nathaniel content, I waded in with my game plan.

"So, I was talking to your mom last night, and she said you guys went to meet a friend at the bus station."

"Not a friend, silly."

"Oh, right. You know she told me, and now I can't remember."

Nathaniel rolled his eyes again. "Geez, Daniel. Is your brain not working? We were supposed to meet my *grandma*." He said grandma slowly just to make sure I heard it.

"Is she your mom's mom or your dad's mom?"

Nathaniel huffed like he was explaining something to a

two-year-old child. "My mom's mom, of course," he said. "I've never met my other grandma."

"Does your grandma, the one you've met, live here in Las Vegas?"

"No."

"Oh, right. Your mom told me that too. She said your grandma flew in from Denver. Did I get that right?'

"Nope," he said. "You know, my mom says if you don't pay attention, you're not going to get smarter, Daniel. My grandma lives in California."

"*Right*. California. I am always getting California mixed up with Colorado," I said, playing along. "Did you live with your grandma in California?"

"No."

"But you saw her sometimes?"

"No."

"Then it was just you and your mom?"

"No. I lived with my grandpa."

The fact that he said *I* and not *we* stuck out like a unicorn walking down Main Street.

"And your mom didn't live with your grandpa?"

Nathaniel shook his head, picking a crumb of bacon off his plate, putting it in his mouth.

"She would visit me a lot. Well, not *a lot*. Sometimes, when I came home from school, she would be there waiting for me. We would always stay at the house, and my grandpa would order food. Mom liked to bring me presents, but I told her the only present I *really* wanted was for her to stay."

"I don't think your mom told me that part."

Nathaniel was staring at his plate now, pushing it back and forth with his finger.

"So, did you like living with your grandfather?" I asked.

"*Grandpa*," he looked up, and his momentary sadness was

gone. "He's really nice. We spent a lot of time together at the beach. He taught me how to fish this year."

"That's neat," I said.

Nathaniel nodded. "I wish I could've said goodbye to him."

"You didn't get to say goodbye?"

Nathaniel shook his head. "Mom said there wasn't time. She had to wake me up when we left. I wish I could've said goodbye."

"Well, maybe you'll see him. Maybe he'll come visit you."

"He won't," he said with a finality that made it seem like a law written in stone.

"Well, you never know. Things could change. You know, your mom told me there was a job here. That might be the reason you guys came, but she told me something else, but— Yeah, I think you're right; my brain's not working right. I can't remember the other reason you guys came to Las Vegas."

Nathaniel looked up at me, his face scrunched up in confusion. I thought I'd stepped over the line this time, and he was going to clam up. Veronica must have instituted some unwritten code with her son. It seemed to be one of those "don't tell strangers because it's dangerous" kind of things. Veronica was keeping secrets, and maybe she'd told Nathaniel to watch what he said. Based on that presumption, I *was* not expecting the truth that came out of Nathaniel's mouth next.

"Did she tell you the other reason why we came?"

"She did." I felt bad lying, but I needed to know the truth. It took a moment for Nathaniel to decide whether to tell me.

"Well, I guess I can *remind* you since you forgot. But you have to remember to keep the secret. At least that's what Mom says."

"Of course. I won't tell anybody, and I don't really have

any friends here anyway. Well, except for you and your mom."
I tried to sound casual about it, but I could see that the
secret bothered the boy.

Nathaniel exhaled, gathering up his courage. He looked
me straight in the eye and said, "The other reason we came
here is because my mom is dying."

CHAPTER EIGHT

athaniel's last words haunted me the rest of the day. We walked the Las Vegas Strip, and the boy never complained, even though we must have traveled miles. I replayed our conversation from the diner. There might have been a hint of sadness in Nathaniel's voice. And maybe a bit of resignation that the universe had delivered such an injustice to his small family. I got the feeling that Nathaniel hadn't quite come to terms with his mother's condition. He'd said it with detachment, like mentioning he'd bought a candy bar the previous day.

I think it's fair to say that those words left me in shock. It wasn't because I'd never dealt with death myself. I'd seen more death in one lifetime than any man should have to see in ten lifetimes. His nonchalance towards Veronica's condition bothered me. The boy either didn't know what death meant, or he was trying not to think about it. I did not want to discuss it, so I focused on him instead.

We played the part of tourists, weaving in and out of crowds, dodging porn card slappers. And we ducked through themed casinos to avoid the midday sun. Around two o'clock, the heat, excitement, and all the exercise took their toll on the boy.

Nathaniel turned to me and asked, "Can we go back to the motel now?"

I hailed a cab and we went back to the motel. Nathaniel nodded off as we rode in the taxi, providing me time to absorb the fact Veronica was dying. Either rejuvenated by the sleep in the cab or the cold blast of the A/C in the motel room, Nathaniel returned to his old self. He flicked on the TV, and we settled down to watch an afternoon of cartoons. We never talked again about his earlier revelation.

When Veronica showed up, her face wore the same tired mask that I'd grown accustomed to. I didn't mention what Nathaniel had told me. I needed time to think. I concluded I would gain the clarity I sought only after a night spent behind the scope of a gun.

———

When I rendezvoused with Tom, Jay, and Benji at the same bar where I'd met them, I was happy to see they'd come prepared. Tom had even brought snacks and drinks for me. I'd picked some up along the way, as he'd suggested. Maybe it had to do with how I'd met them, but I'd anticipated they might show up drinking, but all three were stone cold sober and ready to be on the way.

As we drove along in Tom's Jeep, I fell into their conversation with ease. It felt like I was turning a page. The character I'd been days before was now wiped away. This was the new me, a new Daniel. Of course, I remained introspective, but I had become more outgoing. I was part of the crowd, rather than a fold in the shadows.

That night's client was a ranch owner in his eighties with palsied hands. He greeted each of my new friends by name.

When he shook my hand, I could tell there was still plenty of life left in the old man.

"The coyotes come on the property just after dark. I've lost a couple dozen chickens and my granddaughter's new puppy. I won't tell you how upset she is about that. I'd sit out here myself if I could, except for these damn hands." He held them up as if saying the silent curse. I could tell those shaky hands didn't hold the old man back much.

"Tom, I know I said $75 a head, but how about we raise it to $100? I'm so desperate to get those critters off my land."

To my surprise, Tom didn't go for the higher fee, and neither of his friends protested. "We'll stick with the $75 as agreed upon, as long as you don't mind making some extra coffee in the morning. I'm sure we'll more than make up for it by the numbers."

"That's kind of you, Tom. I'll do one better. How about some eggs and bacon to go along with that coffee?"

"It's a deal," Tom said.

With that, we were off. We split into two groups. Tom and I in one, Jay and Benji in the other. Tom handed me a rifle that looked like it had seen better days. Upon further inspection, it looked fully serviceable. Still, when we got to the silo, I pulled an old T-shirt out of my pack, spread it on the ground, and took it apart piece-by-piece.

"What? You don't trust me?" Tom asked, but there was no malice in his voice. I think he was curious.

After the weapon was completely disassembled, I realized my first impression had been correct. The rifle was old, but well-kept, like that perfect pair of hiking boots worn to its user and indispensable on a winding trail in some faraway mountain range. There was a touch too much lubricant for my taste, so I wiped the excess away.

When I'd put the rifle back together, I was confident I could make any shot I took. We'd have to see about that because there was no time to zero the weapon. Tom must've read my mind.

"She's a dead shot at a hundred yards," he said. "Much past that and she flies left. I've been meaning to take it to a gunsmith, but I've been a little busy." He tossed me a box of ammunition, and I inspected each round with care.

Tom watched me again, a knowing smile creasing his face. "Army?" he asked.

"Something like that," I said, loading the two magazines he'd given me.

I didn't really want to go into my past, and Tom didn't press. As the darkness settled over the arid landscape, I scanned the horizon for signs of movement. Then, as the last rays of daylight disappeared over the mountains, the ranch's flood lights kicked on.

Then the coyotes just appeared. They were fearless and hungry. I looked through the scope of my weapon and smiled. There was just enough light to see their gleaming eyes. The coyotes I'd seen in the past hadn't travelled in packs. The most I ever saw were three together. This group was different. The single file of predators fanned out, like an army sends out skirmishers. The Beast inside me clawed. It was the time of the hunter.

In the initial wave, I took down ten. Thinking the night was over, I stood up to stretch my legs.

"You might want to get yourself good and comfortable again," Tom said. "They'll be back in an hour or so. I'd say we got half of them."

I'd never heard of predators coming back so soon.

"You sure they'll come back?" I asked.

"At first I didn't get it either, but yeah, they do."

We settled in again. Just over an hour later, they were back and the slaughter was on. We killed thirty-six coyotes in all. Tom had designed the perfect kill box. If one pair of shooters missed, sending the coyotes running, it afforded a perfect shot to the other team. All told, I got twenty-one. Tom got eight, and the rest were tagged by the others. I'm not sure what I expected, but there was no squabbling over who had rights over the others. It was done in a civilized manner. It was like they'd done it a hundred times before. There was, of course, the natural ribbing that came from such adrenaline-driven events such as hunting. As we piled the last carcasses into the rancher's old pickup, the four of us basked in the knowledge that we had done a good job.

For breakfast, we drank syrupy black coffee, and we feasted on half-inch thick bacon and eggs cooked over easy. The old property owner must've already eaten because he just sat back and listened to our tale.

"I think Daniel had taken down five before they even knew what happened," Tom said happily. "It was all I could do to keep up."

Jay laughed. "You should have seen Benji. When that first shot went off, he jumped three feet in the air."

"Hey, I've gotten better," Benji protested. "I got more last night than I've ever gotten before. Three," he said proudly, holding up a trio of digits.

Benji shot the fewest, but neither he nor they seemed to mind. It just seemed to be the natural order of things. When we'd gotten our fill of breakfast, the owner handed Tom an envelope stuffed with cash.

"I'll let you know if more come back, but I'm sure things will be quiet around here for a while," he said while shaking Tom's hand. He took the time to say goodbye and express his gratitude to each of us on an individual basis.

I was the last to receive a handshake. The others were already through the door when the owner pulled me in a little closer. He looked into my eyes, saying earnestly, "You're different from the others, Daniel. I can see that. I just want you to know that I understand. I've been there. I want you to know if you ever need help or want someone to talk to, you know where I live."

Then he let go of my hand, and the spell was broken. I wondered what had just happened. Why did it feel like the old man had somehow looked into my soul and found its cupboards bare?

CHAPTER NINE

"You look like you just saw a ghost," Tom said as I slid into the passenger seat of the Jeep.

"I'm just tired," I said, quickly fastening my seat belt, locking my eyes straight ahead.

Tom didn't press, and I offered no further explanation.

The ride back into town was uneventful. Jay and Benji were soon snoring in the back, and Tom hummed along with the Top 40 radio station.

Once we rumbled into view of the city again, Tom asked, "Do you have a way that I can get in touch with you? We might have another job or two in the upcoming days."

"Maybe it's best if you give me *your* number," I said. "I'm kind of without a permanent phone number right now."

"Here," he said, reaching into his pocket, pulling out his business card.

I took the card. I was surprised to see Tom's grinning face on one side of the card with his contact information on the other side.

"You're a real estate agent?" I asked.

"Guilty," he said. "It's not a bad gig. I schedule showings

when I need to, leaving my nights open to do stuff like this. You know, if you're ever interested in trying something new, I sure could use the help."

"What about them?" I said, pointing to the two snoring forms slumped in the back of the Jeep.

"Jay works construction, and Benji, well, he's not really the 'get a steady job' type."

I'd never thought about real estate before. I thought it was a business for silver-haired ladies who drove around in Cadillacs.

"It's my dad's company, but he's mostly retired now. When I got out of the Army, he was happy to have my help. I specialize in land sales, which keeps me away from the concrete jungle. I don't know what I'd do if I was cooped up in the city all day."

"I know how you feel," I said. "I appreciate the offer. I'm not sure if I deserve it, but—"

"I have a hunch you'd fit right in," Tom said. I could see that he was sincere. He wasn't just trying to recruit someone who could do his grunt work.

He was looking for a partner, and I wondered what he saw in me. Apparently, he saw something in me I didn't see in myself. Just under my calm façade, I felt broken, like something less than a man. But maybe, just maybe, this was the fresh start I wanted. This might be the opportunity to take a step in the right direction. As we rolled into town, hope buoyed my spirits—it was a new day.

I soaked in the feelings of warmth and acceptance until we pulled into the motel parking lot. Everything changed when I saw angry yellow flames roaring out the windows of Room 211.

CHAPTER TEN

A s I stood in the parking lot watching the motel belching black smoke and flames, I barely heard the wail of the fire trucks as they quickly approached. Someone grabbed my arm, but I couldn't peel my eyes from Room 211—Veronica and Nathaniel's room. For a long, heart-wrenching moment I contemplated running into the fire to reclaim Nathaniel's tiny body. What did remain of my sanity knew no one could survive the inferno.

Small details appeared in my vision like the world was coming back into color. Black smoke indicated the use of an accelerant. I spotted the familiar Cadillac in the parking lot. The fire fighters pushed me aside as they raced to control the blaze.

I scanned the crowd looking for Meaty Forearms and Shaky Leg. *It had to be them.*

"Hey, was your stuff in there?"

It took time for Tom's question to register.

"No, I've got it all right here."

If every last belonging I owned was in that room, it wouldn't have mattered. As the first streams of water hit the blaze, doubt crept into my mind and then flooded my chest. I relived the scene on the bus where I had met Nathaniel for the first time. Then I had insisted on helping Veronica, offering them a place to stay and a warm meal.

What if Veronica had been right? What if I'd stayed out of her personal business? What if she'd made it to her job, and she had somehow figured out how to take care of Nathaniel?

The firefighters were getting closer now, gaining the upper hand over the dancing flames. Four rooms had been engulfed, but they knew what they were doing.

I tried to push the doubts away while watching the scene unfold in front of my eyes. There were more details I needed to register.

The night shift desk clerk was talking to a firefighter wearing a blue uniform. The cops showed up, doing their best to keep onlookers at bay. I was so engrossed in the scene that I hadn't noticed the motel clerk pointing at me. Then another man, most likely the fire chief, looked in my direction. Naturally, the gazes from the policemen followed, and soon I found myself surrounded. I was peppered with questions: Had I been the one who'd left a lit cigarette or maybe an appliance unattended? When was the last time I'd seen the residents of Room 211? Where was I when the fire started?

I heard what they were asking, but I couldn't tear my eyes from the motel.

I wanted something to fight. I grabbed and clutched my hands, stuffing down my primal need to wring someone's neck. I wanted to punch my fist through a skull. My eyes whipped to where the Cadillac had been, but now it was gone. *How had I missed that?*

"Sir, we need to take you in for questioning," the policeman was saying.

Nathaniel, Veronica. The men in the Cadillac. Meaty Forearms and Shaky Leg.

Then someone yelled from within the bowels of the motel. The focus shifted from me to the announcement. Two firemen leapt into the hot flames and the smoke obscured their forms as they entered Room 211. It didn't take them long to come out. The brave firefighters must have been told to check for bodies inside. The firemen exited the room. One firefighter held up a hand, his fist balled, and he extended two fingers.

"Two bodies," I heard one of the cops say.

The motel clerk chimed in. "There was a kid and his mom staying in that room." She said it with zero remorse. She sounded more like an understudy, happy to have an opportunity to say her line.

Two bodies.

I imagined Nathaniel's withered form, his joints compressed from the intense heat. I had seen burnt bodies before, and I would never forget them. I felt my insides churning, and I couldn't tear my eyes away. I wanted to run up the stairs to see for myself, but I didn't have the chance.

I barely heard someone saying something nearby. Then I felt the cold steel cuffs snap on my wrists. My head turned and I saw the lips of one of the policemen moving. I couldn't hear what he was saying, so I refocused. He was reading me my rights. I saw Tom, Jay and Benji watching with concern etched on their faces. But it didn't really matter anymore, did it?

Take me in or leave me; it doesn't matter.

They put me in the back of a patrol car and left me there as the fire lost the battle it had waged. No one seemed to notice the grief washing over the man sitting in the back of the police cruiser.

CHAPTER ELEVEN

I'm not sure how many questions they asked me before I trusted myself to speak. The police officer assigned to interrogate me was a woman, and she was not unkind. She was definitely going with the whole "innocent until proven guilty" approach. At that moment, I felt anything but innocent. In my mind, sitting in that chair that day, I felt that I was the guilty party. I might not have lit the flame, but my actions put players on certain paths that resulted in the deaths of both Veronica and Nathaniel. A sane man would have given the police something resembling an alibi.

I remember clearly the guy, Meaty Forearms. His name was Wayne. I didn't know Shaky Leg's name, but the duo would be easy to spot. There was no sense doing the police's legwork for them. I had other plans.

"Your friends say you weren't there. Do you want to tell me where you were last night?"

"Friends?" I asked, the first words coming out in a tone of incredulity as I blinked through the haze.

"Yeah, your three friends; they followed us over to the station."

It took me some time to realize that she meant the guys I'd gone hunting with.

"They're not *really* my friends," I said.

"Okay," the police officer said slowly. She must have seen that I was struggling. "Your *acquaintances* said that you weren't at the motel this morning or last night."

"Then why do I still have these cuffs on?" I asked.

"I can take them off if you'd like."

I shook my head. I didn't trust myself; if she did remove the restraints, I didn't know what I'd do. It was better to be chained like an animal. Maybe it should have occurred long ago. Why hadn't an enemy sniper's bullet hit me? Why hadn't a mortar round ended my life? Or why didn't a machine gun riddle my body until I was nothing but bloody pulp on the desert floor?

"Witnesses say two men entered the room that you rented," the cop said, "Do you know who they were?"

"No," I said, although I knew exactly who the culprits she was referring to were.

"You know, things would go a lot smoother if you'd answer my questions. You were in the military, right?"

I didn't answer her question.

"I was in the Air Force," the cop said, "Military Police. I'm in the Reserves now, so I've done some time overseas. I guess what I'm saying is that I'd like to help you."

She wasn't going to get an answer from me. The whole "we both served at the same time" shtick wasn't going to work. I felt anger building inside me, and knew that I would soon need to release it. But not here. And not now.

"Can I leave?"

"The motel clerk said that you knew them."

"Knew who?"

"The mom and her son staying in Room 211. We know

that you paid for the room. The clerk said that she might have been your sister."

"They weren't my family," I said.

"Well, either way, I'm sorry. If you give me your phone number, I'll make sure to call you with any information we get."

She walked around the table and released me from the handcuffs. I had the feeling that she was going to cross the line. I panicked thinking she would put a hand on my shoulder and say, "It's going to be okay," but she didn't. *Lucky for her.*

The door of the room opened and another cop stepped inside. He whispered something into the female officer's ear. They both looked at me, followed by further whispering.

The male cop left, and my interrogator said, "I think you'd better sit down, Mr. Briggs."

"You said I could go."

"I have a couple more questions."

"But you said I could go. What's the point of asking me more questions? I wasn't there, you even admitted that yourself. Now, if you don't mind—"

"The two men who were seen entering the room—who were they?"

"I don't know," I said, pushing the chair away from the table.

"You knew them, didn't you?"

I didn't answer. I played my cards close as I headed for the door.

"Who were they, Mr. Briggs?"

I reached for the door handle, and the cop didn't move to stop me.

"I don't know who they were," I lied.

"Then why do we have a witness saying that he saw you talking to them two days ago at the motel?"

I froze, turning slowly. "If you really thought I'd done it, you'd be putting those cuffs back on. Now, unless you're going to charge me with something, I think it's best if I go."

I went back to the door and opened it.

"We're going to find out the truth, you know," she said.

I shrugged, because it didn't matter. At least not now. But then I realized that it did matter. The cops couldn't find out, because I had things to take care of. The Beast nodded in agreement. If it could have smiled, it would have beamed; I'd just promised it blood.

I left the interrogation room behind and strolled through the police station. Tom was waiting for me.

"How did it go?" Tom asked.

"Fine. Could you give me a ride back to the motel?"

"Sure, no problem."

His friends were waiting in the Jeep, and they didn't ask me about the interrogation when I stepped into the car.

"If you need a place to stay, you can always crash with me," Tom said, starting the Jeep, "I've got plenty of room."

"I'll be fine, thanks. I just want to get my deposit from the motel, and then I'll be out of your hair."

Tom nodded, and we pulled away from the curb. My brain was clicking away with plans falling into place and supplies tallied in my head. I was so caught up in my own little world that I almost didn't see the police car drive by, nor did I sense the flicker of recognition within my subconscious. But The Beast did.

"Stop! I need to get out," I said.

The Jeep slowed. Before it had rolled to a stop, I jumped out. I started running back toward the police station. The police cruiser I'd seen headed for the fire lane. The cop seated in the passenger's side got out first and opened the back door. Nathaniel and his mother stepped out into the sunlight.

CHAPTER TWELVE

The closest I can come to describing the feeling of utter relief was total peace, complete tranquility, an immense letting go, like Earth's gravity had been multiplied thirty-fold and then released. I don't know how I stayed on my feet.

Nathaniel was all grins when he stepped out of the police cruiser. When he saw me, his head cocked to the side as if he didn't recognize me. I had assumed the two bodies they talked about at the motel were the boy and his mother's shriveled forms forever encased in a crispy exterior. I'd imagined him crying and banging his ineffectual fists on the motel door as the flames and the intense heat overwhelmed him.

But it hadn't been him because I was watching him walk towards me. It took all my will to remain standing and not fall to my knees.

Then I saw Veronica. She was talking to one of the cops that had brought them to the station. During a sideways glance, I noticed her disfigurement. There was an angry scrape on her left cheekbone. She was nodding to the policeman but staring at me. If I had been at the top of my game and not dog tired, I might have noticed there was something more in her stare – was it hostility? But at that moment, I was just relieved they were alive.

"Hey, Daniel, we got to ride in a police car," Nathaniel said.

"That's, um, pretty awesome."

"Yeah, they said you were here, and they wanted to talk to Mom about the fire."

"I'm glad you're okay," I said.

"Do you know what happened?" he asked. "The policeman said something about electricity, and Mom said it was an accident."

The way he said the word 'accident' had the same effect as an ice-cold glass of water splashed in my face. My self-awareness snapped back, and I felt a sense of clarity returning. Then my yin slapped my yang, and I sensed the adrenaline waning. I realized I'd gone two straight nights without sleep.

Accident. I guess it could have been an accident. I looked from Nathaniel to his mother; they both still stared at me.

It took a couple hours for the police to take Veronica's statement. They didn't ask Nathaniel anything, because he hadn't been anywhere near the motel. According to him, he'd been with his grandmother. In fact, Veronica had been with them also.

"Where does your grandmother live?" I asked as we waited on an uncomfortable bench inside the police station.

Tom had left to take Jay and Benji home, but he had promised to come back to give me a ride.

"She's staying at a hotel, and guess what, Daniel? We got to order breakfast in the room. They brought the food to us, and yeah, you were right, I really like French toast. I ordered French toast, and they put strawberries on top with lots of syrup."

That gave me an idea.

"What did your mom have to eat?"

"Oh, she didn't eat."

"She wasn't hungry?"

"No, she left for a little bit. She had to go to work or something."

Then he was on to the next topic, flitting from one random subject to another in the way kids' minds work.

As I listened, I thought about how I could dig deeper to ferret out the truth. Had Veronica really gone to her job? It was possible. Maybe there was more training she needed, or maybe she had to pick up her uniform.

Then there was the grandmother. What role did she play in all of this?

They were questions that would have to be asked later, because my energy was sapped. What I needed most was sleep, but that wasn't an option as long as I was sitting in a police station.

The same female cop who had questioned me, escorted Veronica back to her son.

"If we need to talk to you, we'll give you a call," the policewoman said. She then noticed my presence and said, "Oh, Mr. Briggs, I didn't know you were still here. Looks like you've made a friend."

"Me and Daniel were *already* friends," Nathaniel corrected her.

"My apologies," said the cop. Then she snapped her fingers. "That reminds me—do you like pirates, Nathaniel?"

"Maybe," he said, his face dubious.

"How would you like to stay at a hotel that has pirates *and* a pirate ship?"

"Are they good pirates or bad pirates?"

"Oh, they're good pirates."

"Sure, as long as my mom can go," Nathaniel said.

"Yes, of course she can," she turned to Veronica. "I know the manager of the hotel. It's called Treasure Island. He's going to put you guys up in a room until you can find a new place to stay."

Veronica could have shown her gratitude by saying, "Isn't that great, honey?" or, "Wow, that's really nice of you to do that for us," but she didn't. She just stood there in her listless manner, looking even more tired than before.

"Can Daniel come with us?" Nathaniel asked.

"Yes, you didn't think I'd leave him out, did you?" the cop said.

"That's really not necessary," I said.

"Call it professional courtesy. Besides, every once in a while, an Airman gets to take care of a Marine. Am I correct?"

I nodded, at a loss for words.

After the way I acted in the interrogation room, I was clueless about why she was helping me.

"By the way, I never got the chance to formally introduce myself, Mr. Briggs. My name is Verelli, Sandra Verelli."

She stuck out her hand, and I took it in mine.

"Please call me Daniel, and thanks for the hotel room. That is really nice of you."

She held my hand for a moment, looking at me as if there was something further she wanted to say. She released my hand and said, "If there's anything else you guys need, you know where to find me." Then she turned on her heel, returning to her other cases.

"Well, what do you say we go find those pirates?" I asked, trying to sound upbeat. Nathaniel didn't catch the weariness in my voice.

"Yeah. Do you think they'll have French toast there?"

"I bet they will."

As we left the police station, Nathaniel was thinking about food again, and I contemplated how I would interrogate his mother.

CHAPTER THIRTEEN

Ask most people, and they'll tell you that they can't remember their dreams. Sometimes they'll remember the last thing, or maybe the highlights, but they never remember the whole dream.

The manager escorted us to our rooms. It turned out to be adjoining suites at the pirate-themed hotel and casino. My head barely hit the soft pillow when I plunged into the dream world. I tried pushing the dark images away. I begged and pleaded for a restful slumber. Instead something sparked up ahead like a match in the darkness. I couldn't resist the call. In my dream state, I walked toward the light.

I came upon a scene that was both familiar and inexplicable. There was a crackling fire nestled in a small depression in the dirt. I took a seat, like I'd been invited, and my dream body complied with the silent order before my brain could resist. I looked around the fire and saw familiar faces. They were men I'd served with. Some had been lost during battle. Others were still alive, as far as I knew. They might still be in The Corps, or maybe they were out now. They all were talking, laughing, making jokes, but I couldn't hear their words.

There was one kid in particular, who entered and left the Corps with the rank of private. He was one of those rug rats who had always been in trouble because trouble always seemed to find him. But he was always the first one to take a lagging Marine's pack should it become too heavy. He was the kind of guy who would throw a forty-pound medium machine gun over his shoulder, although he had long ago tipped his weight allowance. For some reason, in that dream I couldn't remember his name. He was chatting away like he always had, making shapes and gestures with his hands, describing sexual acts from his latest conquest, and the rest of the Marines were all laughing.

Then the images from that dream were gone, swept away like sand during a powerful storm.

I opened my dream eyes, and I was walking again. This time I heard the crackle of gunfire, familiar booms of exploding artillery shells and close air rockets. There was a foul odor in the air. I immediately recognized it as the stench from the open sewers mixed with the carnage of the ongoing battle. It was a smell you couldn't quite get away from while fighting in the Middle East.

I strained to see the war raging ahead, and I watched it play out before my dreaming eyes. It was as if someone had flipped a light switch. This act of my life I remembered vividly, maybe because it was the first time I'd ever saved a unit from an ambush. In the way of dreams, I could see everything as it had happened. I had a bird's eye view, like I was literally flying overhead. I also saw it through my zoomed in rifle scope, and my vision scanned back and forth between these two views.

The Marines on the front lines were yelling for more ammunition, calling for reinforcements and close air support. They were close to being overrun. There was a familiar crack followed by another. One Marine turned his head and pumped his fist. I couldn't hear what he was saying, but I read his lips, "*Snake Eyes*," he said. The name passed on down the line, and the defensive positions held.

Bloodied Marines screamed, firing back at the enemy with their nearly exhausted supply of ammo. *Crack, boom, crack.* Over and over. I spotted my old rifle, and I could almost feel the concussive shock from the barrel, the kick of the butt against my shoulder. I listened for the calm voice of the spotter in my left ear.

There were so many targets: heads, torsos and legs. Any piece of human flesh I saw, I reached out with my weapon and touched with deadly accuracy. *Snake Eyes.* That's what they'd called me.

Then, like the scene around the fire, this one blew away.

And on it went as I continued dreaming. The dream leaped through both good and bad memories, through trials and triumphs. The dead mingled with the living. It was an accurate portrayal of my life. I got the feeling someone had gone through my life and made a highlight reel. It was now playing at the base theater for all to watch.

It left me feeling raw and naked. Feelings long since buried were again exposed, ripped from my heart and soul. As I walked, I attempted, in futility, to not observe the scenes as they unfolded. The death overwhelmed me and was almost too much to bear as experiences were unwittingly yanked from my brain. But I eventually noticed a pattern. Death was always quickly followed by a ray of light that would push its way through the darkness.

When I came to the end of that dream, I saw the old rancher's face again. He was the one who'd said he understood, that he knew me.

His eyes were shining like a million bits of glitter reflecting the afternoon sun.

"I see you," the voice said. "I see *you*."

Then a hand reached out and, with a single finger extended, touched my chest.

"I see you," the rancher's form said again.

Then, like the rest of the dreams, he melted away with his arm still extended.

The light never came back. While I floated back to consciousness, I was left to ponder the meaning of my dreams.

CHAPTER FOURTEEN

I woke up in a pitch-black room. It took me a few moments to realize that it wasn't the middle of the night. Somehow, I'd managed to close the blackout curtains the night before. Had it been nighttime when we'd arrived at the hotel? No, it had been daylight.

The clock on the bedside table read 4:00 pm. Had I really slept almost twenty-four hours? My mind was riding that funny line between mush and clarity; when you are aware there's a tangible idea, however you're still too groggy to make sense of anything. I took my time. Instead of ignoring the scenes I'd experienced in my dreams—like I normally did —I tried to embrace them.

After the longest shower of my life, I stepped out feeling somewhat whole again. I wiped the steam from the mirror, and I found myself gazing at a stranger. My beard had grown thick, and my blond hair was now hanging well past my ears. Gone were the days of the regulation high and tight, but I didn't mind much. Maybe this was the new me—a working man. But working for what?

The truth. I needed to find the truth. That search began with the woman staying next door to me in the motel.

Now dressed and scrubbed clean, I went to the door to the adjoining room and knocked. I waited with no response. I knocked again, and I thought I heard rustling from the other side. Maybe I'd awakened them. But the person who answered the door was neither Nathaniel nor Veronica. It was a woman I didn't recognize.

"You must be Daniel," the woman said, looking every bit like she had just stepped off the cover of a *Southern Living* magazine. She had a tasteful amount of gray in her hair, and she had the kind eyes of an elementary school librarian.

"I'm sorry. I was looking for Veronica."

"She took Nathaniel to breakfast. He wanted to wait for you, but—"

"Yeah, I was asleep," I said.

"Feeling better?"

"I'm sorry. I don't mean to be rude, but who are you?"

"I'm Veronica's mother."

This was Nathaniel's grandmother? I didn't quite get a grandmother vibe from her. One assumes wrinkles and maybe a full head of gray hair when conjuring up the image of a grandmother. The woman standing in front of me didn't fit that image at all. If I'd met her on the street, I would have pegged her at forty years of age - tops. She was fashionable without being overtly so. She must have sensed my confusion, because she explained.

"I'm Veronica's stepmother. I get that look a lot."

"Oh, right." I said quickly.

"Veronica didn't tell you, did she?"

"Your stepdaughter doesn't talk much," I said, "Would you mind if I came in?"

Nathaniel's grandmother opened the door wide and ushered me to a couch where Nathaniel's belongings were spread with a kid's panache. I moved a couple of things aside and sat down.

"I'm Margaret, by the way," she said.

"Sorry, I—"

"Didn't mean to be rude?" She finished for me with a smile, as if she'd expected my awkwardness. "Veronica says you're a man of few words."

She's one to talk, I thought. *It's time to answer some questions, lady.*

"Nathaniel says you're just in town for a visit." I asked.

"Yes, I just wanted to make sure they got settled alright. My stepdaughter has had kind of a hard time getting adjusted in the past. She's had some issues that date back to high school, so I thought it was only right that I meet them here."

She made it sound like Veronica had moved to Las Vegas to work at a customer service center. I decided to push my luck. The time for tiptoeing was over.

"Did she tell you what happened?" I asked.

"She told me that you helped her, and that's enough for me. I don't like to get involved in the details of Veronica's life. I've found it's easier to let her know I'll always be here if she needs help. I can't count how many times I tried to barge my way into her life and gotten pushed back out the door."

"But you were aware of her new job—the one she came here for?"

"Of course."

"You don't see anything wrong with her bringing along her son – your grandson?"

"Why is that wrong, Daniel? Because *you* think it's wrong? If there's anything I've learned from Veronica's trials, it's that she is her own woman. She will do what she likes with her body. I'm no saint either."

How could she be so impassive? They might not be blood, but they still were family. How could she just stand by knowing her stepdaughter would be defiled by countless men? I didn't know whether to storm from the room or scream obscenities.

"I can see that you don't approve, Daniel, and I appreciate that. It means that you care. Veronica needs good people in her life."

"But what about Nathaniel? Don't the two of you think about the long-lasting effects this might have on him?"

"Do you think me so crass that I would allow my grandson to be swallowed up in Veronica's world? She loves that boy, and I do too. I will do anything to make sure he's safe."

"While you're living up the high life in some new hotel, you're allowing them to live in a beat-up motel with a stranger?"

Margaret exhaled as if she'd been repeating the same argument countless times over. "I offered them a place to stay. Veronica declined, and she begged me not to tell Nathaniel. I have respected her wishes. She's run before, and I can't risk that again. She may not be blood. But she is my daughter, and Nathaniel is my grandson. If you're going to sit there and judge us, feel free to leave any time."

We just sat there silent for a couple of minutes. She wanted me to leave, but I wasn't about to go. The truth pulled me back.

"What about your husband? Nathaniel says that his mother took him away, and he didn't get to say goodbye."

"Is that what you're worried about? Do you think that Veronica stole her son? First of all, he's my *ex-husband*. Second, he knew she was coming to get Nathaniel, but he didn't want to see her. He didn't want to see what she's become. I assume by now that you know Veronica is sick. I tried to get her to tell me what it was. I think it's cancer, but I can't be positive. She's always been a little thinner than the rest of the girls. She has never been one to take care of herself. Actually, in the beginning I thought it was just another phase she was going through."

"That still doesn't explain why Veronica wanted to work at The Frisky Filly. Hell, the second day here she got a job working at a hotel. There's plenty of work to go around."

"She told me," Margaret said.

"None of this makes any sense."

Margaret shook her head sadly. "I'm afraid that's the way the majority of Veronica's life has been. It may not have driven the wedge between my ex-husband and myself, but it definitely was the last nail in the coffin. It's hard to explain to someone who hasn't been through it. I have watched Veronica make the most inexplicable decisions, putting her life on the line. She put our family in danger. And all for what—the next high or the next thrill? I won't pretend to understand it, Daniel, but I've chosen to be here to support her and Nathaniel in much the way you have. Don't get me wrong, I will not stand by and see that little boy get hurt."

"Why don't we stage an intervention or—?"

"It won't work," she interrupted, "We've tried it before. It's never one thing. When we took Veronica to a psychiatrist, he listed every malady ranging from bipolar disorder to pathological lying. He had the nerve to tell me that Veronica was a nut he couldn't crack. Those were his exact words. Can you imagine the gall of him to say she was a *nut he couldn't crack*? I could have slapped the irony out of his mouth. Needless to say, we never went back to see him again. But there were other specialists over the years. Some tried to help, while others didn't. She was a special case, or "pet project" for a few, but most often she was a hard case for others. During this time, it felt like she was just slipping away. So, when she called, asking me to come, I dropped everything and I flew here. I hoped that this might be the time things would change."

"What about your ex? Maybe we can get him here. Maybe the two of you—"

Margaret shook her head with such resignation that I ceased talking.

"You still just *don't* understand, Daniel. And frankly, if I didn't know the truth, I wouldn't understand either."

"What am I not understanding? Your daughter needs help. Nathaniel needs help. *We* need to help them. Just get on the phone. Call your ex, and we'll do this together."

"No," she said emphatically, "*He's* part of the problem."

"But I thought you said—"

"He is a good man, and he loves Nathaniel. He always wants the best for Veronica. But if his daughter tells him to jump, he will ask her how high."

"But what if he sees that this time he can't go along? What if he understands that he has to fight for her?"

Margaret slumped in her chair and mumbled something so softly I couldn't hear her.

"What?" I asked.

Then, after regaining a measure of composure, she looked me dead in the eye and said, "You don't understand. Her father's the one that made sure she got the job at the whorehouse."

CHAPTER FIFTEEN

I read comics as a kid, and Superman was one of my favorites. For a time, there was an ongoing storyline about Superman's polar opposite who lived on Bizarro World. It was a cube-shaped planet that was supposed to be the strange stepsister of Earth.

That's how I felt—plunged into Superman's Bizarro World.

"You've got to be kidding me, right?" I asked Margaret.

"No. I know how it sounds. But my ex-husband is *not* a bad man. You have to believe that. We are good people just trying to do the right thing for our daughter. While I don't agree with his decision, I do think it came from a place of love."

I coughed out a laugh. "Love? That's not love. That's probably *the* most twisted father-daughter relationship I've ever heard of."

Margaret looked down at her hands in her lap. They were devoid of a wedding ring, but I noticed her stroking the place where it would have been. There was no white line so the divorce must have occurred some time ago. She didn't have any answers for me now. There was no way she could convince me that the level of support she and her ex-husband had given Veronica was okay. Based on my moral radar, this was way out of bounds.

"You *all* need help," I said. "If it were up to me, you'd all be committed."

Margaret just nodded as if she felt the same.

The hotel room door opened. This cut off any further explanations from Veronica's mother. Nathaniel ran inside while his mother strolled in behind him. When he saw me, he said, "Hey Daniel! Did you really sleep that long?"

I swallowed down the anger threatening to consume me. I didn't want Nathaniel to see that, because this situation wasn't his fault.

"What can I say, kid? I was beat."

He plopped down next to me on the couch. "This place is *awesome*. Mom said we can eat whenever we want. Can you believe that?"

"That is very kind of the hotel manager." Margaret said it in the way that parents do, sounding as if everybody should stop what they were doing to write the manager a thank you note.

"What are we going to do today?" Nathaniel asked, oblivious to his grandmother's condescension. "Can we go to the pool? Can we?"

"Honey, you don't even have a bathing suit," Veronica said. Her body language was even more languid than before.

Nathaniel's question gave me an idea.

"Hey, I need to pick up a bathing suit, too. Veronica, why don't you and I run to the store? Nathaniel, you can stay here with your grandmother and watch television."

"But I want to go with you," Nathaniel said, looking between his mother and me.

Veronica didn't say a word, so I answered, "I need to talk to your mom to see if she can get me a job where she's working."

"Hey, that's a great idea!" Nathaniel said, bouncing up and down. "When I visit mom at work then I can visit you, too. That'd be so cool!"

"Okay. You wear a Size 2?"

"No," Nathaniel said. "Size 6," rolling his eyes, as if I were the dumbest person on the planet.

"Right, sorry," I said, "You want a pink bathing suit, right?" Again, Nathaniel rolled his eyes, and I raised my hands in mock surrender. "All right. Definitely no pink."

Veronica didn't say a thing as we rode down the elevator and walked through the lobby. She kept silent as we traversed our way through the endless casino. "I think they've got some things in the gift shop up ahead," I said.

Fifteen minutes later, we bought a swimsuit for each of us. Veronica actually offered to pay. When she presented the credit card, I caught a look at the name on the card. It said *Margaret Taylor;* it was her mother's card.

"It's mighty nice of your mother to be paying for all this," I said as we left the store.

"That's what she does. She thinks it will make me happy. To be honest, right now I just don't have the energy to fight her. So, yeah, I'll use her credit card."

"How are you feeling?"

"Mostly tired," Veronica said with a shrug.

"Margaret told me about your father."

"Oh?"

"She said you are close." Veronica shrugged noncommittally. "Veronica, you need to tell me what's going on."

She stopped and turned to face me. "Look, I'm not in the mood. I want to go upstairs and get Nathaniel changed into his new swimsuit. What I don't want to do is listen to you provide me a checklist on how to be a good daughter and how best to take care of *my* son. So, if you don't mind, I'm going up to my room, alone."

She started walking away from me. I called to her, "She told me that your dad helped you get the job you came to Vegas for."

Veronica froze, and with exaggerated slowness, she turned around to look at me with spite. "What did you say?"

"You heard me. But that's not all. Nathaniel told me you're sick. He said you're dying. I'm here to help if you want it, but there can be no more lies."

Veronica shook her head like she was trying to get my last comments out of her brain.

"You have no idea what you're talking about."

"Then why don't you tell me? I'm all ears, Veronica."

I watched her as she searched for the right response. Her eyes darted back and forth as if she were reading a scroll held out in front of her. Then she looked at me with her eyes narrowed.

"Why did you have to come into our lives? Do you think you can rescue us? Is that your deal? Is that what you do? Travel from city to city and play the knight in shining armor? Well, let me give you the lowdown. My life stinks; it always has. Nathaniel is the only thing I've got. I've met guys like you before. I know all about you, and this time, you don't get to help. This is none of your business. *We* are not your family."

"What about Nathaniel?" I asked. "Is this any way for him to live?"

"He is *my* son. He's not your responsibility," she snatched the plastic shopping bag out of my hand. "I think you'd better leave before I call that female cop. I'll tell her you're harassing us. From what she's told me about you and your past, I bet she'd love to add harassment to your record."

I had no idea what she was talking about. What had Sergeant Verelli told Veronica? I'd assumed Veronica had also been interrogated at the police station. Never had I thought there was sharing of information occurring. Sergeant Verelli had just made it to the top of my "I need to talk to" list.

"Maybe I should call Sergeant Verelli myself," I said. "I think she'd like to know why you came to Las Vegas. I'm sure there's child endangerment somewhere in this messed up tale."

Veronica actually laughed. "She knows why we came to Las Vegas. Working out of such establishments in Nevada isn't a crime, Daniel. Welcome to the real world—I can use my body in any manner I choose. And you have no claim to me or my son."

"Then just tell me one thing. Why did you bring Nathaniel here? He would have been better off, and happier, staying with your dad. Even though he looks like he's having fun, I can tell that he's scared. Do what you want with your body, but keep Nathaniel far away from your lifestyle."

"You just don't get it, do you? This is *not* your business."

"Explain it to me," I snapped.

The stare she leveled at me hovered somewhere between condescension and pure hatred.

Atta girl. Get riled up, I thought. *Show me your cards.*

"We came to Las Vegas because there's a specialist here who can help."

"What, like a doctor?"

"Yes, like a doctor," she answered, her voice dripping venom.

"Good, you're going to get help?"

She laughed and the sound actually caused people walking by to turn her way. She appeared strangely maniacal.

"You sure are a humble son of a bitch, aren't you? You think after spending a couple hours with me and my son, you know everything about us. Let me tell you the real reason we came to Las Vegas. We didn't come here for me, and we sure as hell didn't come here for that job. *Nathaniel* is the one who's sick. The only person who can help him works in a hospital three miles away."

CHAPTER SIXTEEN

Veronica's words left me cold. I just stood there as she left. No doubt she thought she had finally dealt with the problem known as Daniel Briggs. She wasn't going to let me see Nathaniel again. But some way and somehow, I *would* see him. I would not let my sorrow for the boy eclipse what I had to do next. I just couldn't shake the feeling that something else was going on. It was like there was a picture in my head, and the only clear image was the center line that dissected the left side from the right. The sides became increasingly blurrier, but I was certain there was something else there. No matter how hard I concentrated, I just couldn't see it.

Veronica would be no help for the time being. I could press the grandmother, but she was squarely in her step-daughter's corner. The last thing I wanted to do was march into that suite and cause a scene in front of Nathaniel. He was just a kid, and I wanted to spare him from the screwed-up relationships of adulthood a little while longer.

Veronica had given me one piece of information that I could work with—Sergeant Verelli. The policewoman needed to explain why she'd shared my personal information with Veronica. Then maybe I could leverage that into looking deeper into Veronica's past.

A short time later I found myself standing in front of the police station. Other than the three cops dragging in a pair of unruly drunks, the place seemed quiet. I went inside and asked for the Sergeant.

Fifteen minutes later, she joined me.

"Sorry," she said. "Busy day. How can I help you?"

"I have some information for your investigation."

"Why don't we go to my office? Do you want anything to drink?"

"Water would be great, and coffee, if you've got it."

"This is a police station. We'd have a mutiny on our hands if we didn't have coffee at all times."

I did not share in her laughter.

Sergeant Verelli looked tired. It was the kind of exhaustion you see in a person putting in extra hours to get a tough job done right.

Her office was a cubicle. The room was designed to be entirely economical except for the single office, belonging to the lieutenant or maybe a captain. Otherwise, there were no solid interior walls, and the entire office area looked like one big bull pen. I wasn't fond of police stations. It's not that I dislike cops. I like good cops, and there are plenty of those. It was just that every time I ended up in a police station, I was usually right in the middle of a shit sandwich.

"Sugar or creamer?" she asked.

"Black, thanks," I took the mug from Verelli. "Any leads on the fire victims?" I asked between sips of coffee.

"No IDs as of yet. The coroner's still working, but he did say both vics were male. One had a recent knee replacement. That should give us some insight, maybe a serial number. But we're at a standstill until the DNA results come back and the coroner gives us his report."

I wondered if anyone had filed a missing person report. I really wanted to ask if there was any visible trauma left on the bodies, but I figured she probably couldn't tell me that, regardless of professional courtesy. After all, the police were in the middle of an active investigation.

"I wanted to talk to you about Veronica Taylor," I said.

"It's a shame about her."

"What do you mean?"

"She has cancer. My mom went through chemo a few years back. It's the hardest thing I've ever seen, and I've seen some horrible things, you know? It's even more difficult when that person is family."

I nodded, thinking of Nathaniel.

"Did she mention anything about her son?" I asked.

"What do you mean?"

"Did she mention anything about him being sick?"

"I don't think so," Verelli said, genuinely surprised. "Is he sick?"

How much should I tell her? I decided to go with the truth.

"Yeah, she told me he is. And I think it's bad."

"God, I hate it when that happens to kids. Is it cancer, too?"

"I don't know. She wouldn't tell me. She's a little—well, I'm not exactly her favorite person right now."

Verelli cocked her head and said, "That's strange. She had nothing but good things to say about you when she was last here."

"Are you serious?"

"Yes, I'm sure. She went on about how you helped her on the bus and how great you are with her son. She made you sound like a modern-day Robin Hood." She paused and stared at me for a moment. "I can see that surprises you."

It did.

"Let's just say our last conversation was anything but cordial."

"I'm sorry to hear that. Maybe it has something to do with her illness. My mother had mood swings that would drive me running from the house one minute and sprinting back the next. It's really hard to predict. Maybe she was just experiencing one of those episodes."

It was time to turn the tables. "She said you told her about me."

Verelli set her chipped coffee mug onto the desk and looked at me with incredulity.

"Excuse me?"

"She said that when we were here for questioning you told her about my past."

"She was the one talking—not me," Verelli said. "I think you've got your facts twisted."

"No, she told me that *you* told her about me. I want to know why and what gives you the right to tell a complete stranger who I am and what I've done in my past."

Verelli's face reddened. *Good, I was getting to her now.* The words that came out of her mouth were anything but the concession I had expected.

"I'm not sure what kind of cop you think I am, but I *don't* divulge personal information to someone I don't know. Other than a quick check of your records for outstanding warrants, I don't know *a thing* about you."

"But when I talked to you, I got the feeling that you had pulled my official record. Maybe you called St. Louis and talked with someone there."

"I don't know what you think you heard. I extended the whole military courtesy thing to you only because that's what I try to do for all veterans. You came in here looking like you'd just been put through the ringer. So, yeah, I was being nice. But I did not tell Veronica Taylor anything about you."

"Why would she lie? She said you told her."

"Look, I don't have time for this. I promised I would provide you the same courtesy I allowed you the other day. That is why I agreed to see you today, but I am too busy for this. I've got two bodies at the morgue to handle plus another seven missing persons' cases to solve. Unless you have some information pertinent to the fire you witnessed, I suggest you leave *now*, Mr. Briggs."

I probably should have said I was sorry or something, but I wasn't in the mood. I just gave her a curt nod, and I got up and left.

I was no closer to any answers, yet it felt like the very real danger lingering on the horizon had picked up steam. It was getting closer, and I wasn't prepared for when it touched down. I still needed to grasp the entire picture. For that to occur, first I needed to assemble the pieces of this increasingly difficult jigsaw puzzle.

As I walked out of the police station, my mind churned through every fact I could recall—Veronica's illness, two dead bodies in a burning motel, Veronica's father, Nathaniel's illness. How did they all tie together? None of it was making sense.

What also made no sense a second later was the screeching sound of turning tires, and the sight of a familiar Jeep tearing down the street, headed straight at me.

CHAPTER SEVENTEEN

I stood in the middle of the road, daring the vehicle to come closer, and as it hurtled my way, I realized that maybe this was it. This was my moment. This would be when my life would finally be snuffed out.

Then the vehicle jogged a bit to the left, and then back to the right, overcorrecting. I couldn't see the driver's face, though I did see the top of someone's head. Was it Tom? It was his Jeep, but why could I only see the top of his head?

The overcorrection to the right put the vehicle off course, and as the Jeep flew by, I saw Tom slumped in the driver's seat with a splash of red on the left side of his skull. I turned and ran after it. The Jeep jumped the far curb, narrowly missing a pedestrian, eventually slamming into the brick wall of a vacant building. The airbags deployed with a puff. In the time it took to reach Tom, the air bags were already deflating. Tom's body was slumped toward the left, and it was hanging halfway outside the Jeep.

He was the only occupant. I went to work extracting him from the wreck. His seat belt was stuck. No matter how hard I tugged, I couldn't pry it from him. Soon, there were people surrounding me. Police officers arrived from the station, and Sergeant Verelli handed me a blade.

"Here, cut the seat belt with this."

I had to move quickly now. There was a lot of blood, so much that half of Tom's face was covered in it. Once I was through the seat belt, I returned the blade to Verelli, catching Tom's body as the seat belt gave way.

"Call an ambulance," Verelli ordered her men. She bent down assisting me in examining Tom after I had lowered the wounded man to the ground. "I can't see where he hit his head." She was putting on a pair of examination gloves and handed me a set.

"That happened before the crash," I said.

"How do you know?"

"I saw him as he drove by. I'm pretty sure he was unconscious."

"Well, he's breathing and his pulse is strong," Verelli said. "I'm going to take a look at the vehicle. You keep him stable." I nodded and she headed to the Jeep, shifting the deflated airbag aside, looking at the front seats as well as in the back. She made a full turn.

"Anything?" I asked.

I thought that maybe there would have been a wedge on the accelerator that had kept the Jeep in a forward trajectory. It was possible that Tom had passed out upon seeing me, but why had he been coming here? It was impossible for him to know where I was.

"This is your friend, the one that accompanied you before, correct?" Verelli asked, continuing her search of the vehicle.

"Yeah," I said, "His name is Tom. Here's his card."

I slipped Tom's card from my back pocket and handed it to her.

"There's an office number on here. Is there someone I should call?"

"Maybe you should; he said he worked for his dad."

Just then, the ambulance showed up with its lights flashing and siren wailing. The EMTs were methodical, preparing their tools before kneeling down next to me. They began a preliminary examination of Tom.

"So, you didn't see him hit his head?" one of the medics said.

"No," I answered.

"The gash looks pretty deep," the medic said, probing the wound and covering it with gauze. "We won't know if he's had real head trauma until we get a CT, but you're welcome to ride along if you'd like."

When the medic said "you", he was referring to Sergeant Verelli. I wasn't family. That much was obvious.

"I think Mr. Briggs should go, if that's okay with you."

The medic gave me an up and down glance, and then he nodded his approval.

With precise movements practiced over thousands of cases, the two EMTs shifted Tom onto a backboard after they secured his neck with an immobilizer. Then he was carried into the ambulance, and the gurney was locked on the center track.

I took a seat next to him, not really knowing why I was going other than the fact it seemed Tom had been coming for me. Besides, if I went to the hospital, maybe Jay and Benji would show up to tell me what had happened. I also hoped that Sergeant Verelli could get into contact with Tom's dad. Maybe one of them would have the answers, because answers in my life seemed to be on a prolonged sabbatical.

"I'll have them dust the Jeep for prints, just in case," Verelli said, "Then I'll meet you at the hospital. He may not be awake for a while, but I'd like to be there. When he does wake up, I'll take his statement there."

The anger from our earlier conversation was gone. She was all professional now, even sympathetic in my presence.

"Thank you, Sergeant, and about before—"

Verelli waved away the apology. "It's fine. I understand. This has all been pretty upsetting for you. Take care of your friend, and I'll see you in a few minutes."

She gave me one of those "everything's gonna be okay" nods and then closed the ambulance doors.

We pulled away from the scene of the accident, and I realized Verelli had never searched Tom's belongings. Instead of insisting the driver stop, I performed my own cursory search from head to toe. There were no marks other than the one on his head. Then I touched his pockets, the front two and then the back pockets. It was awkward getting around the gurney straps, but I did it. On the search of the last pocket, I was rewarded with a rectangular piece of paper, thicker than a regular business card, and embossed in raised lettering. The card was a tasteful shade of pink and had a logo I instantly recognized: The Frisky Filly. There was no phone number, no name, just an address.

Is that where Tom had been attacked? I'd never told him about the place so it made no sense. My mind wandered down a darker path. Could Tom be part of the whole thing? Was Tom, Jay and Benji's plan all along to get me away from Vegas on the hunt for coyotes to leave the motel room unguarded?

No, that didn't make sense because what about the two bodies? Veronica and Nathaniel were still alive, so maybe that meant—

That's when Tom squeezed my hand, softly at first, and then more urgently. He opened his eyes. They were large and bright. His lips moved but no sound came out. He was moving his mouth like someone who had lost their dentures or like his lips had been sewn shut.

"It's okay. We're taking you to the hospital," I said. He tried to shake his head, but he winced in pain. His lips cracked open and he said something I couldn't hear over the sound of the ambulance chugging to get to the hospital.

I bent down and put my ear next to his mouth. In a voice that sounded like he had marbles in his mouth, Tom said, "They took Jay and Benji. I think they're dead."

With the word "dead", he let out a great exhalation. Then he lost consciousness again. A split second later, the alarms on the monitor he was attached to started beeping.

The EMT in the passenger seat turned my way, "What happened?"

"I don't know. He woke up, talked for a second and then he passed out."

The paramedic released his seat belt and slipped into the back, checking the monitor. Then he checked for Tom's breath sounds and pulse.

"Damn it," he said, and he got into position to begin performing chest compressions.

CHAPTER EIGHTEEN

Tom's vital signs stabilized when we arrived at the hospital. The EMT sat back, wiping his forehead with the back of his arm. The doors of the ambulance opened, and as the hospital staff helped pull the gurney out of the ambulance, the slightly winded EMT rattled off everything he knew about Tom's condition. Everyone was professional. Nobody questioned my presence or said anything to me. They quickly whisked Tom away for further examination.

Once the EMTs had retrieved their gurney, they came back. The one who'd saved Tom's life said to me, "The waiting room is around the corner. Good luck."

There was really nothing else to say. He didn't know me or Tom. For all I knew, Tom was the tenth person he had saved that day. He reminded me of the Corpsmen we had in the Marine Corps. They were good men—professional, always looking out for their Marines. They were our protectors in a very different way than I protected them. While I reached out with burning lead, killing the enemy, the Corpsmen provided a healing halo to those injured.

There was no way I could do that job, because I needed to fight back.

"Thanks again for everything," I said to the EMT. He nodded and patted me on the back as if to assure me everything would be okay. I then went in search of the waiting room.

———

AFTER REPEATED attempts to obtain information from the hospital staff, I resigned myself to waiting. A few minutes later, an older version of Tom rushed into the waiting room. In an instant I knew he was Tom's dad. He had a deep tan, and he looked like he'd just left the golf course.

"Excuse me, I'm looking for my son," he said to the triage nurse at the plexiglass window.

"What is your son's name?" she asked.

Tom's father told her. "I'm his father."

"Yes, sir. Ah yes, here it is," she said, clicking away on the old computer keyboard, "I'll see if I can get a doctor out here to talk to you."

When he turned away from the nurse, I saw the anguish on his face. I didn't know the man, but I stood and walked over to him.

"Are you Tom's dad?" I said. He looked up, surprised.

"Yes. Do you know Tom?"

"Sir, my name is Daniel Briggs, I'm—I guess you could say I'm one of your son's friends."

The father searched his memory for a minute. I fully expected him to say, "Daniel who?" Instead, he said "Oh, yes, Tom told me about you. He said you might be a good fit for the company. You're new in town, right?"

In that moment, I couldn't respond. When Tom had

mentioned looking for some help for his real estate company, I had assumed he was just being nice. But he'd actually talked to his father. I'd never been one who sought or enjoyed compliments, but for some reason the fact Tom had talked to his father about me validated my reason for coming to Las Vegas.

That feeling was dashed after I remembered where I was standing.

"They just took him in to get checked out," I said, not really wanting to tell Tom's father that his son had almost died on the way to the hospital.

"Were you with him when it happened—you know, the car crash?"

"No sir, I was...well, I was at the police station. I was just leaving and Tom's Jeep crashed not far from where I'd been standing."

"What? I—I don't understand. That doesn't make any sense. How did he crash? Did someone run him off the road?"

"No, I think he was injured. He had a head wound. I think he was unconscious before he ran off the road."

"My God," Tom's father inhaled sharply. "I need to have a seat."

We walked to the waiting room, where I'd been sitting, and he lowered himself shakily to the couch. He was murmuring to himself as if replaying something in his head. Then suddenly he turned to me and asked, "Are you sure you don't know anything further?"

"No, sir. I hadn't seen Tom since...I guess it was yesterday. He took me on a coyote hunt."

"Sure, sure. He told me about that. But, he said he was going to see you."

That was news to me.

"I honestly don't know anything about that."

"We were at the office. I remember because I was just leaving. I'd forgotten my clubs and Tom was on the phone. He looked agitated. He hung up the phone, got up from his desk. He asked me if I could lock things up on my way out. I asked him if there was anything wrong, and he said: 'I have to find Daniel.'"

We sat there for a couple of minutes, each analyzing the situation in our own ways. *Why had Tom needed to see me?* Maybe it was about Jay and Benji. But what about after that? Had he been attacked on his way to find me? The deeper I analyzed the situation, the bleaker it became. I searched for answers, but instead I found only questions—so many questions!

Then I remembered the card I'd shoved in my pocket. I pulled out the pink card and held it up to Tom's father.

"I found this in Tom's pocket. Do you know why he might have had it?"

"The Frisky Filly? No, that's not Tom's cup of tea."

"Are you sure?" I asked, needing to ask the question.

"Tom and I are quite close. We have been ever since his mother died. I'd know if he went to The Frisky Filly. Plus, you've met him. He's not really the type that needs to buy something like that." Then he paused as if he'd just remembered something.

"What is it?" I asked.

"I totally forgot. Tom helped them buy the land where they built The Frisky Filly. He knows the owner." *Jackpot*, I thought. "Do you think they had something to do with this?"

"I don't know," I answered honestly.

I didn't get a chance to ask another question because, just as I opened my mouth, the doors to the adjoining emergency room slid open. Veronica Taylor stumbled inside, carrying something in her arms. It looked like a bundle of clothes or maybe a bag.

But when I stood, I saw what it really was. It was Nathaniel's body, limp and bloodied, his face an ashen mess. My legs started moving before my mind could catch up, and I saw Veronica swoon. I wasn't close enough to catch her. Her eyes rolled back in her head, and her body slumped forward. Nathaniel fell to the floor.

CHAPTER NINETEEN

The hospital staff reached Veronica's and Nathaniel's prostrate bodies before I could. It was almost as if they'd been expecting that very thing to happen. Strong and sure hands pushed me away from the horrific scene. Veronica's body appeared intact. She had blood covering her shirt and hands from where she'd been carrying Nathaniel. In contrast, he was literally covered in blood. There was so much, it was difficult to determine the source.

As they rushed him out of the entryway, I thought I had glimpsed a gash over his right eye. But then he was gone, behind the doors. I could have pleaded until I was hoarse. But they wouldn't allow me back to see him because I wasn't family. To the hospital staff, I was just another stranger.

I paced so hard you would have thought my boots would crack the tile floor. I walked heel first, like recruits on the parade deck pacing endlessly back and forth. One by one, people around me were being taken away, but by whom? None of this made any sense, and I pounded across the floor. In desperation, I tried to crack the code, but I just met more questions. There were plenty of unknowns, but slowly my vision adjusted. I kept coming back to a single common factor or point of intersection—the card I'd found in Tom's wallet.

The Frisky Filly was Tom's former client, and it was also Veronica's contracted employer. I realized that was where I had to go. All signs pointed there. I said a quick goodbye to Tom's father, promising to be back, and I headed for the door.

I was so intent on leaving the place that I almost ran headlong into Sergeant Verelli.

"Sorry," I said quickly, trying to move around her, but she stopped me with an outstretched arm.

"How's your friend?"

"I don't know. No updates on his condition yet. I'll be back in a few minutes; I just need to get some fresh air," I lied. I decided I wasn't going to tell her about Veronica and Nathaniel. She'd figure it out soon enough. There was no need to delay my progress.

"Okay," she said, "I'll catch you when you come back."

She had mistaken my preoccupation as grief. Even the crassest person provided someone time to grieve. I smoothed down my shirt as I walked, trying to make sure I was somewhat presentable. I didn't have time to go back to the hotel.

The time for picking up scraps of information was over. It was time to go straight to the source. I hailed a cab. As I slipped in, the driver asked where I wanted to go. With urgency, I said, "The Frisky Filly."

The place was well outside of town. It was far away from onlookers, nestled in a small valley. As we took the last turn leading to The Frisky Filly, I almost asked the driver if we were headed to the right place. I had expected some squat brick building with bars on its windows.

The establishment looked more like a weekend spa with open grounds. I heard the familiar *tick, tick, ticking* sound of sprinklers. The sprinklers were on in an effort to prevent the desert heat from scorching the emerald green grass. Now that I thought about it, maybe this all *did* make sense. Tom's father had mentioned his son had sold the property to the owner; Tom was in the land business. The location was perfect for private interludes.

"Looks like you're a little early," the driver said, giving me a deadpan look. He pointed to the parking lot which was almost empty. "I've never been here myself, but I hear it's classy."

I probably should have engaged with him further. Instead, I just sat there watching the approaching scene. Once we arrived at the portico, a female with light brown hair and an easy smile opened the door of the taxi. I had expected a large and heavily muscled man wearing an ill-fitting suit to greet me.

"Welcome to The Frisky Filly," she said. I handed the driver his cash and grunted my thanks.

"Have fun, buddy," he said, laughing as he drove away.

A woman at the front door handed me a cold towel that smelled of mango, or was it papaya? I unfolded the towel, wiping my face and then my hands. Then I returned the towel to the girl.

"Enjoy your stay," she said. She grabbed the towel with black tongs and deposited it in a bucket. The brunette who'd opened my taxi door escorted me inside.

"Is this your first time to The Frisky Filly?"

"Yes."

"Welcome." I was then handed off to someone else with a quick, "Enjoy your stay."

I'm not sure what I had expected—most likely what I'd seen in the movies. I expected to see half-naked girls making eyes at me, puckering their lips, and puffing out their chests. That image was not what I experienced. Of course, there were pretty women, but they were all tastefully dressed. Some wore sundresses while others chose to wear skirts and tops. Based on their choice of apparel, I would have thought they were working a job in an office setting or maybe going out for a picnic. This did not resemble a house of ill repute. But I was a rookie, so what did I know?

The next handler took me to the check-in desk.

"Welcome to The Frisky Filly," said an older woman from behind the counter.

You could tell she'd been very beautiful at one time. Her voice was welcoming and her eyes were kind. The staff reminded me of the mythical Sirens who lured hapless sailors from their boats with their beautiful songs. I needed to play along without falling for the temptations. The woman at the counter slid something to me which I picked up.

"We have a variety of options for you to choose from, but my girls don't do anything kinky. If that's what you're looking for, I'll be more than happy to pay for your cab fare to get back to town."

She had given me a menu of services which included massages, facials, and even steam baths. Patrons could buy a couple hours of companionship, or they could spend a full night with one of The Frisky Filly girls.

"Do you see anything you think you might like? I'm happy to help you choose."

I thumbed through the menu nervously. It was one of the first times in my life that I felt completely out of place. I pointed to something in the middle of the list.

"Will you be paying with cash or putting this on your credit card?" she asked, taking the menu from me.

"Cash please." I found it interesting that she never asked my name. Maybe complete anonymity was a freebie not mentioned on the menu.

"We have an ATM in the lounge if you happen to need more funds."

I shook my head, grabbing the wad of bills from my pocket. She didn't even blink, likely accustomed to guests carrying lots of cash. She took the money, counting it out carefully. She then handed back my twenty dollars change. Then she smiled.

"Can I ask how you heard about us? You must be new because I don't recognize your face. I like to keep tabs on where our advertising is working. There is no sense wasting money, you know?"

She said it like she owned a Domino's Pizza, and she was worried about the money she'd just spent on posting an ad in the local newspaper.

I decided to press my luck. "Tom Hoover told me about this place."

Her face brightened. "Oh, Tom! He is such a nice young man. He helped us find the land you're standing on, you know? He really took care of us when it came to the negotiations. The former owner was a devil of a man, but Tom helped see the deal through." Then she must have realized that she'd gone too far, crossing the line of anonymity. "I'm sorry, you probably weren't interested in all that."

"No, actually I am," I blurted, "I might work for Tom."

"That's fantastic!" She reached out and touched my hand. "If you're one of Tom's friends, you must be nice. You can imagine some of the types we get in here. We try to weed them out. It's not always easy."

"Maybe it has something to do with the name of your business," I said.

She shrugged as if she'd thought about that, but didn't really care. "You have to market somehow. For some reason, the thought of a pretty pink pony elicits the response we're looking for. Now, if you'd like to follow me to the lounge, the girls should be waiting."

I don't know the reason for what I did next, but I stopped her with an urgency born of necessity. I asked, "How do you know Veronica Taylor?"

The woman's eyes narrowed, glancing up to the camera, where someone was definitely watching.

"*You* know Ms. Taylor?" she asked. She looked at me again as if for the first time. I wondered what she saw. Then she smiled again, her calm façade plastered back in place. "Now, Tom's friend, I don't want to alarm you, but momentarily some very large men will come out of that door. If you go with them quietly, they won't hurt you. But if you don't, well —. We don't want things to get nasty now, do we?"

CHAPTER TWENTY

She was true to her word. Moments later, two muscle-bound men appeared, dressed casually. They could easily have been mistaken for body builders, all mass and focus. They were clean-cut with no visible tattoos. They appeared right at home in this small setting, despite their disproportionate size.

I replayed the events that had just occurred. When I had mentioned Tom's name, the owner had been happy to have me as a patron compared to the 180-degree turn in her demeanor toward me after I'd mentioned Veronica's name. I couldn't help but wonder whether Tom's injuries hadn't been levied by someone at The Frisky Filly.

We took a narrow hallway void of any human traffic. When we arrived at the office, I was surprised to see how small the office was. The furnishings were quite sparse. There was a simple desk cluttered with papers, a framed poster of the Las Vegas skyline being the only concession to decorating. Completing the look were two chairs—one behind the desk and one in front. I took the one in front and the bodyguards squeezed in behind me.

The owner waited until I was settled before taking her own seat behind the desk. "Now, tell me how you know Ms. Taylor."

"Does it matter?"

"Yes, it does. *Ms. Taylor* is not among my list of favorite people currently." She sounded like a teacher addressing a child who was disturbing the rest of the class.

"Why, because she decided not to work for you?"

"That's none of your—" Then I saw the spark of recognition. "You're the young man from the bus station, aren't you?"

"And what if I am?"

The revelation actually made her grin.

"It all makes sense now. You protected her then, and you're trying to protect her now. Your one mistake was coming here because this is my stomping ground, not hers." For some reason, she regarded Veronica as a rival.

"So, if it's not about the contract, what is it about?" I asked.

Calmly, as if it really didn't matter, she said, "This is about my men who disappeared. Ever since that girl came into my life, I've had nothing but trouble."

"Then why did you hire her?"

"I probably shouldn't tell you this, but her father asked me to hire her, as a favor."

"Do you usually get references for potential hires from their parents?"

"Of course not. That's what made me listen. He said he would guarantee her contract. If she slipped away, he would buy her out." It was obvious that she now regretted the accommodation.

"Why would you send those two guys after her? You knew you were going to get your money."

"They got a little carried away, I'll admit that. But it

wasn't until that little hussy came into town that everything went wrong. That's what I get for doing someone a favor."

I chuckled darkly. "You call hiring a man's daughter so that you can fill your pockets with hundred-dollar bills a favor?"

The woman actually snorted. "I don't know how much money you think we make, but it's really like any other business. We suffer the same volatility. Some weeks we struggle; other weeks we do very well. I don't have suitcases full of hundred-dollar bills that I take to my international banker every month. Veronica was an interesting case. Yes, I'll admit receiving her father's call was a little bit disturbing. It wasn't until after he explained his reasons that I decided to go along."

"What did he tell you? What was the reason he gave?"

"He said she was sick—she had some sort of terminal cancer. I'm not sure which type. He said that although she was sick, she didn't really appear that way. Aside from having to wear a wig and suffering from the occasional lack of energy, she appeared to be fine."

"I didn't know The Frisky Filly was an outlet for the *Make-a-Wish Foundation*," I said.

The words came out without thinking. I was actually focused on the two bodyguards standing behind me. I could see their reflections in the glass framing the poster of Las Vegas behind her.

"I'll admit it doesn't sound like something I should have done. But sometimes you get a client with a specific taste. Ms. Taylor's father seemed to know this. People have their fetishes, and long as they're not obscene, who am I to judge? Now, like I told you in the beginning, we don't do any strange things around here. If a man or a woman wants to spend time with a woman dying of cancer, who am I to deny that? She would never be hurt, and she would be paid well. I pride myself in the way I take care of my girls. They even have free health care. "

I barely heard what she was saying. The Beast was coiled, ready to strike. It was impossible for the other people in the room to know the real danger I posed. I was sitting comfortably in the chair, and outwardly I appeared completely relaxed and at ease. If the owner wasn't going to give me the answers I wanted, I'd have to go find them.

"So, you run a freak show?" I asked, trying to goad her.

She shrugged. "Call it what you want. I'm a business-woman. When I see a need, I try to fill it. How's that different from anything else you've seen on the Las Vegas Strip? My girls don't smoke, and they're not allowed to do drugs. They're clean and taken care of."

The phone rang. She glanced at it like she would ignore it. This was my time—the moment to spring.

She grabbed the phone, "Yes. Okay, patch her through," she said with reluctance.

I gauged the distance between me and the two muscle heads. I'd have to get creative, but that wasn't necessarily a bad thing. Then the owner did something unexpected. She looked at me while continuing the conversation. Whoever was on the other end was talking about me.

"Yes, *officer*. We'll hold him here until you arrive." She put down the receiver and smiled at me. "Well, it looks like you've been busy."

I didn't answer, waiting for the flicker of her eyes that gave her men the signal to take my arms. I was ready.

"You come in here accusing *me* of taking advantage of Veronica. To be honest I'd forgotten about her boy. Just for the record, I would *never* hurt a boy. Nobody in this establish-ment would lay a finger on a child."

"What the hell are you talking about?" I asked.

"That was the Las Vegas Police Department. I think you

are familiar with Sergeant Verelli? She's an old friend of mine. According to the sergeant, our lovely Ms. Taylor has accused you of attacking both herself and her son. It looks like you're the one who has some explaining to do."

With that telltale flicker of her eyes, she signaled her men. Time slowed; The Beast made its move.

CHAPTER TWENTY-ONE

My head started the momentum, throwing my body backward in one fluid motion. The two security men had really done all the work. It was impossible for them to know what I was. Under all that hair and dust I was not human. In that moment, I was something primal, and the piece of humanity left in me was but a flicker.

I unleashed The Beast's chains.

It's arms—my hands reached out and grabbed the comically slow guards, each by their shirts as I fell backward. They were strong and provided the perfect leverage, not for me to arrest my movements, but to allow my legs and, more specifically, my knees to fly backwards in the beginning of a crushing somersault, like a gymnast doing a backflip.

Their movements had already assisted me, but my pull linked them in. At almost the same time, my knees connected with their surprised faces. Both men staggered, temporarily stunned, while I found my footing. My body was loose and nimble, ready to strike again, if necessary.

And strike it did.

A sweeping roundhouse kick caught one in the temple

and then I spun around, catching the second man with a headbutt to the sternum. Neither blow would be deadly, but both men were out of the fight.

The owner of The Frisky Filly stared at me with shocked eyes, but she recovered quickly, reaching for the phone. I slapped it out of her hand, and it crashed into the wall.

"Don't hurt me," she said quickly. She was no novice to violence, I could see that. She was wary, but not afraid.

"A way out. Now!" I ordered, pointing to the door.

She took one last look at her men on the ground and nodded, walking purposefully to the door. "Front or back?" she asked.

"Back."

I had to give her credit. She had kept her cool. Maybe she had been mugged or robbed before. There was no telling what she'd endured, given her chosen profession. Under different circumstances, I might have actually respected her, but right now, all I needed was a way out.

The place was larger than I thought. We passed girls who said "Hello" to their employer, and the owner played along.

"Faster," I said. I imagined the police closing in. It wouldn't be long now and they would be at the front door.

"If I go much faster, someone will notice," she said. Of course, she was right. "Why are you doing this?"

"You didn't exactly give me a choice."

"Then why did you do it?"

"Do what? Take out your guys?"

She didn't answer as another pair of girls walked by, chatting happily. It wasn't until we were out of earshot that she said, "No, the kid. Why did you hurt the kid?"

"I didn't hurt a kid. Someone has the wrong side of the story."

We passed six more doorways and the entrance to the pool deck before she said, "You don't look like the type."

"You don't know my type, lady."

"I've seen all kinds," she said, still walking briskly. "You could have hit me, but you didn't even try. It probably would have been the smart thing to do. Taking me was a risk."

"I needed a way out."

"Of course you did, but you could have figured that out on your own. Despite what you might think, I don't have an army of bodyguards marching down the halls to save me. And what you did back there? I don't know if an army of body-guards would have even helped." It was a strange time to pay me a compliment.

"Just keep going," I said. We took one final turn, and then she pointed to a door marked "Exit" with one of the green illuminated signs designed to stay on during emergencies and power outages. "You're coming with me," I said.

"Do you really want to turn this into a hostage situation?"

A voice came over the hidden intercom system. I recognized it instantly to be Sergeant Verelli. She ordered the resort's inhabitants to congregate in the center courtyard. Her voice was calm and respectful.

"That's one day of business shot," the owner said.

I almost wanted to ask her if the police stopped by often looking for runaway girls or escaped felons. I was neither, so I didn't ask.

"There's a car out back. A grey Jaguar. The keys are under the seat. Take it."

I didn't understand. "Why are you helping me?"

"If it gets you out of this place quickly maybe my customers won't leave."

"As soon as I walk out that door, you're going to tell them which way I went, aren't you?"

"Of course I will. But I'll give you a five-minute head start."

I gave her a look that made it obvious that I doubted her.

"Look, it's obvious that something's going on here. Two of my men are missing. Now a good kid like Tom is lying in the hospital, not to mention the boy they say you attacked. Now, I'm not that good of a judge of life choices, but I'm a good judge of men. I could see when you first asked about Tom that this was personal to you. That's why I'm taking this personal. Take the car, and get to the bottom of this. Here," she handed me a miniature business card that looked more like a metro train ticket, "That's my private line. If you need my help, call me."

Without any other words to say and The Beast roaring for us to leave, I said the only thing I could think of, "Thanks."

She nodded, crossed her arms, and leaned against the wall. She winked and gestured with her head to the door. This time I complied with her suggestion.

CHAPTER TWENTY-TWO

I got as far as starting the owner's Jaguar before I stopped. Sure, I could make an easy getaway, but then where would that leave me? Where would I go? If I was on the run, I would not get the answers I sought.

This time, instead of chains, I had to use an iron cage to contain The Beast. The bars were as thick as my biceps. It howled in protest. I gritted my teeth, and white-knuckled, I grabbed onto the steering wheel. I attempted to tamp down the urge to flee. I wanted to live to fight another day.

"No," I growled at The Beast, and I got out of the car. I replaced the key fob where I'd found it. With each step, the tension in my body fell away. Up to that point, my life's history had been full of violence. All I knew was kill or be killed. I was still human and, at my core, I was compassionate. But I knew there was something lacking. There existed a disconnect that continuously launched me headlong into danger. Time after time, I'd welcomed it. Heck, I'd even called for it.

Why had I come to Las Vegas? Had it been the thrill of excitement or the thrill of a dirty fight? I think it had more to do with the people who surrounded me—those who had been hurt.

I'd always taken the blame, but *this* was not my fault. I had to believe that, or what was the point? How could you live with yourself if you believed everyone else's pain happened because of you? The two dead men in that burnt out motel room—the disappearance of Jay and Benji—Tom lying unconscious in the hospital ICU room—and Nathaniel. I'd done everything in my power to help him, and yet, the world had still thrown its accusations at my feet.

It was time to stop running. Feeling *touched* by The Frisky Filly's owner had been the final straw that broke my previous convictions. She also saw something in me that I was unable to see in myself.

How strange is that to say? I know how the words must sound. As I walked, my steps picking up steam, they sounded as foreign as an alien language. *You are something better*, I told myself. The voice was small and much like the shy child in the back of the classroom who could barely be heard above the ruckus of fellow classmates. I had been lucky too many times. Was it by chance I'd made my own luck, or was it something else?

I didn't know for sure, but I had this overwhelming feeling that my luck had run out. Unless I shifted my path, my actions would only lead to further destruction. I had to trust in others as they'd trusted in me. As I made the final turn leading to the front of the plush gentleman's resort, my resolve solidified. I raised my hands over my head, indicating surrender, when I came into view of the police officers.

"I'm not armed," I said.

I saw one of them speak into his shoulder mic. He then put his hand on his sidearm. The Beast whined. I could still get away. They wouldn't shoot me if I ran, but I was done running. I stopped fifty feet from the confused gathering.

They were obviously waiting for Sergeant Verelli. A moment later, she emerged from The Frisky Filly. She was the first to extract her weapon, and the rest of the officers followed suit. They now surrounded me as if I were a dangerous criminal.

"I'm not armed," I repeated.

Verelli didn't say a word.

"On the ground!" one of the officers ordered.

I complied. I lowered myself, first kneeling down on my knees, then down to my chest, hands palm down and extended. Over and over, The Beast howled, ordering me to run and fight - anything other than laying in submission on the hot pavement. I ignored its screams, instead focusing on remaining stock still.

This had to be the way. One arm after the other was yanked down as someone slapped handcuffs on my wrists. I focused on the cold steel, requiring a focal point to distract me from The Beast.

I probably still could have gotten away if I wanted. It had been my last chance, but I hadn't taken it. *You are strong, and you will get through this*, I told myself. But then somebody above me bent down. Sgt. Verelli, in a steel-cold sounding voice, barely above a whisper said, "Daniel Briggs, you are under arrest for the murder of Nathaniel Taylor."

CHAPTER TWENTY-THREE

I couldn't speak, even after they had thrown me in the back of the police cruiser and we were well on our way toward the police station.

Murder? My compulsions from a few minutes before weren't even a memory. Nathaniel was dead. That sweet little boy—curious and fun-loving. For some reason, the only words of his that keep coming back to me were, "French toast. French toast." Nathaniel would never eat that again.

Then came the image of Nathaniel lying on the hospital floor. He'd been covered in so much blood that I remember thinking that he'd been dunked in a barrel of it. It didn't make any sense, but then none of this did.

I wanted to struggle, to kick and scream and pull at my restraints. I should've demanded an explanation, but all I felt was a deep, resounding sorrow. The feeling enveloped me so completely at that moment, staring out of the police car window with vacant eyes, I resolved at the earliest opportunity to take my own life.

After all, what was it all for? I'd tried to do the right thing. I tried to stand up for those who couldn't stand up for themselves. Look where it had gotten me. No—where it had gotten Nathaniel! He was dead—murdered. Gone.

The tears came before I knew they were falling. Losing a friend or family member was one thing, but the loss of any child was heart-wrenching. I felt like I was trying to breathe underwater. Instead of breaths, I gulped gallons of water. I didn't want to live. I wanted death to take me. Death, that sneaky bastard. I'd outwitted him too many times. *No more. I'm here if you want me.*

For some reason, my memory flickered back to my first days in the Marine Corps. I was a newly-minted lance corporal. Our platoon commander, a fresh-faced butter bar straight out of Quantico had been tasked with giving us a brief before we went on liberty. It was in the days before 9/11. No one had a combat action ribbon, except for the old-timers who'd been around for Desert Storm. There were also the lucky few who'd returned from some back-water conflict that nobody could talk about. Death was as foreign to us as a green alien from Mars. I'm not sure why I remembered that brief. In it, the lieutenant warned us about the dangers of depression, alcohol, and suicide. Most of my fellow Marines weren't even listening.

"There's a reason the success rate of Marine suicide is higher than all other branches," the lieutenant had said. "It's because when a Marine puts his mind to something, he does it. He doesn't pop a bottle of pills; he grabs a weapon, and he takes care of the problem with deadly force."

Much to the lieutenant's dismay he got a couple of "Ooh-rahs" and "Semper Fi's" from his Marines. Those were the days when suicide was still a relatively rare phenomenon in the Marine Corps. Knowing someone who'd committed such an act was rarer still.

I'm not sure why those words stuck with me all this time. Maybe it was the simple profoundness of his words. The fact that when a Marine chose to take his life, he took it. He didn't leave a note, and he wasted no more time. He went through with it with the most terrible precision.

Now, as I sat being jostled back and forth in the back of the police cruiser, I understood. I didn't want to feel anymore. My time was up. I would've gladly given my life for Nathaniel's, but that opportunity had been taken away from me. My hands were empty; my heart was hollow. I felt beaten down. I was so lost in my ocean of misery that I didn't notice when the car rolled to a stop.

I had no idea how long the back door was open, and a voice continued saying, "Daniel, get out. Daniel, *get out!*"

I looked up with bleary eyes to see Sergeant Verelli beckoning me outside. I shook my head trying to clear it. Was I at the police station? All I saw for miles around was desert.

She is going to kill me, I thought. That had to be it. *Good, it's what I deserve.* Take me out to the middle of nowhere. Shoot me and leave my body for the coyotes and the buzzards. It's how it had to be.

"Damn it, Daniel. You need to get out of the car. I need to talk to you."

I didn't answer, but I scooted to the other side of the vehicle and stepped outside. I was ready to wipe away the numbness and pain. I probably should have said something like, "Just do it," or "Make it quick," but I didn't believe I was deserving of a quick death. Instead, it should be drawn out and painful. I deserved an excruciating penance.

"Look, I'm sorry. You really need to snap out of it," Verelli said.

Maybe this was her game. Get me thinking I was safe, and then put me through the numbers. Sure, it made sense. Verelli was behind it. If you were a cop, there were plenty of ways to kill a man, or even a boy. She'd somehow gotten Veronica to point the finger at me. Maybe I should have asked how she did it, but I didn't really care any longer. She'd won and there was no one left to protect. Thus, my job was over.

The slap came out of nowhere, but I took it stoically. I looked her right in the face, begging for more. The Beast clawed, but I battered it back with a thought, the easiest it had ever been to control.

Another slap, this one harder, stung my ear. I just stared at her, slack jawed and unthreatening. All I could think about was that boy and how the lieutenant had been right. Once you got something in your head, you couldn't let it go.

"Damn it, Daniel. You need to tell me why you did it."

"Why don't you just shoot me?" I said. We were alone. It would've been easy, and that was fine with me.

"I don't think that you did it."

Maybe her words should have had more of an effect, but they didn't.

"It doesn't matter," I said. "It's over. I'm done." I felt, rather than saw, her take my handcuffs off and throw them onto the backseat.

"You tell me and I'll let you go right now, but I need your help," she begged. "None of this makes sense."

It's not supposed to make sense, I thought. We spend our lives searching for the shortcuts, groping around in the darkness searching for meaning. We fight our hungers while feeding the pain, and where does it get us? Nowhere.

I thought about reaching for her weapon. Maybe then she would defend herself, but I didn't have the energy. I was tired —so damn tired.

"Your friend Tom is going to be okay. He's still unconscious, but he's going to make it. Veronica needs you right now, Daniel. She's lost her son." Out of all her comments, this is the one that cut through the haze.

"You said she had accused me of killing him," I paused, unable to get the name out.

"She did, but I don't know. I can't explain it. I don't think she meant to. She was hurt too, you know. She's going to be bruised all over her body. Somebody really went to town on her." Verelli wasn't seeing the obvious, and even in my state, I knew that if I was accused and had no alibi, it was very likely that I would be tried and sent to jail. I'd played right into someone's hand. If I had a cap, I would tip it to them with grudging respect. They'd won without giving me a glimpse of who they were or what their endgame was. That person was the ultimate opponent—the winner.

She went to slap me again, but I caught her hand. "Just take me in or shoot me," I said. "You can say I struggled, that I tried to get away. I'm done."

"Look, I know you've been through a lot."

"You have no idea what I've been through," I snapped, barely holding the anger back. "You were in the Air Force, right?"

Verelli nodded.

"Did you ever have to kill anyone?"

"No, I—"

"Then you have *no idea*. I've killed people. I've killed a lot of people, not just over there, but here on American soil. I deserve it, okay? I'm sorry I can't help you. My time is up."

She just stood there in shock, as if she couldn't believe that I would quit. *The joke is on you lady*, I thought, *because I just did*.

"I can't believe you won't help me. Not even for that little boy?"

There was no doubt that she was preparing one last protest, or maybe another slap when the side of her head exploded, splattering me with blood, brains and bits of bone.

She just crumpled like one of those soiled rag dolls falling to the ground. I just stood there.

I couldn't have been frozen for long because I heard the echo. That familiar sound. The Beast knew it and growled at me to do something, and something I did. I bent down to unhook Verelli's pistol from her waistband, but then I stopped. My hands were shaking. Another dead body. Another black mark on my soul. I can't tell you why I did what I did next. I still don't understand it. To be honest, I'm not even sure it was me. Instead of grabbing that gun and putting it to my head, I wiped the blood from my eyes and I stood.

Then I ran.

CHAPTER TWENTY-FOUR

There was no pattern to my retreat. I don't know why the gunman never took another shot. I had to have been an easy target, but the killing blow never came. I imagined what it would feel like. Would it feel like anything? I envisioned stopping, turning to face the shooter, providing a perfect kill shot.

Take the head, I thought. *Take me in the head*. Make it quick and painless. *No, take me in the leg and let me bleed out. Let me bleed for my sins.*

Yes, that's what I deserved. A slow gasp and a mindful agony. My legs never slowed. I ran as if in a trance, like my body was propelled by something other than myself.

The Beast was strangely quiet. I called to it idly to make sure it was still there. It yawned rather than responding with its familiar growl. *Strange*, I thought, but then maybe this was the beginning of the end. While The Beast slumbered, I would die, but I would die willingly.

On I ran. Sometimes I tripped over low-lying brush. Each time I picked myself up, continuing my errant journey. On and on I pressed. On and on my legs took me. I began to feel the thirst. It started as a longing for my old friend, Jack Daniels. My mouth did its best to salivate at the thought. *Yes, Jack, take away the pain. Help grease the way as I enter hell.* But my old friend wasn't there. Gradually, the thirst spread. I needed buckets of water poured down my throat. But again, this was only a fleeting thought of the me that was still present there.

The 'it' that was controlling my body never slowed. I felt like one of those windup toys that you crank until you hear the crack, and then you let it go. It never stops until the winding power is gone. That's exactly what happened to me.

At some point, I saw it become dark, and with a final soft exhale, my body fell to the ground. I gasped and heaved, expelling what little remained in my stomach. I closed my eyes and felt the scorched desert earth on the back of my arms and neck. I didn't care. Was this a sign of things to come? Was it the first inkling of what the devil had in store for me? I was headed to the lowest cell, on the lowest level, in the lowest pit of hell.

That's when I heard them, that funny chattering sound of coyotes. They sounded like babies crying. I probably had enough energy to fight them off.

Let them come, I thought. I'd killed their brethren, and now they were here for revenge. I felt them circling, cautious at first, like a roving band of bandits who'd found a stranded merchant, but of whose lethality they were still unsure.

I saw one set of eyes and then another in the darkness. I imagined them salivating, yearning for the kill. My eyes closed one last time, my lips, mouth; one last kiss to the universe. My heart beckoned the painful death to come.

———

I AWOKE SLOWLY, frightened at what I might find. *Hell?*

The first sensation was an overwhelming thirst. My parched mouth prompted my swollen tongue to lick my cracked lips. My eyelids parted, and I prepared myself for the worst. Strangely, other than the thirst, there was no pain. *How could that be?* I tested my arms and legs, and everything seemed intact. It took a moment before I could roll over onto my stomach and then push myself to a kneeling position.

My head swam from dehydration. It sent a sharp stab of pain into my skull. When I looked down at my body, it too was intact. There was neither a scratch nor a drop of blood to be seen. Then I looked all around me; there was nothing for miles. There were no roads—no signs of civilization—no coyotes. As my eyes cleared, I searched the ground. I saw the truth. All around where I'd been laying were the familiar paw prints of the coyote pack. Round and round they must have circled, but *why hadn't they attacked?*

I was too dehydrated and too exhausted to think, although some part of me recognized that I'd slept without a single dream I could remember. I had not awakened with that always-present sense of remorse, like I'd done something in my dreams requiring confession.

I gave a brief thought to staying, laying back down and letting the sun take me, but ultimately, I decided to keep moving. *Why? I don't know.*

The coyotes hadn't attacked. I could probably give them one more night, find a hole to lie down in and truly experience misery, and then, in the dark of night, I would emerge to make my final payment. I stood on stiff legs, and unlike the run the day before, I felt every step now.

It was my final journey, a final reminder of how fragile the human body is. I accepted it as my punishment, expecting a wave of unconsciousness to claim me at any given time, any given moment. Onward I continued walking toward the hills —the only landmark in my line of sight. Yes, toward the hills and away from civilization, it would be a fitting place for me to die.

When I finally arrived at the foot of the largest hill, I must've been close to delirium. Sometimes my vision doubled, even tripled. There was the ever-present headache, but still I walked. My body was strong, despite the years of abuse I'd put it through. Once, I remember collapsing. I awoke to find a tumbleweed lodged against my cheek. I brushed it away, and it tumbled away on its aimless path. I stood again, looking up at that large hill.

The second time I awoke face down in the dirt, I rose again. This time, as my feet fell into a rhythm, I felt parched and almost giddy, like someone had told me a joke while I dreamed, and I'd awakened with the laugh still on my cracked lips. Maybe I was still dreaming. The world was a blur.

One time I found myself veering off course, traversing the hill instead of ascending it. A quick correction put me on the right path again, only to be veered again in my fugue state. I would have given anything for a shot glass full of water.

I looked up to see the crest of the hill; it was so close now. I pushed on, thinking that this would be the perfect spot to take one last look at the Earth from my high vantage point. From there, I would say my goodbyes, remember the pitiful life I had lived, and remember the lives lost. I must have been babbling incoherently because I felt my swollen tongue moving up and down, back and forth.

Then I was there at the top of the hill—a place to rest.

As I crested the summit, a shocking light as brilliant as the sun fell upon me, assaulting my eyes. I took one final step and planted my foot wrong. I caught the edge of something hard, and I fell forward possibly over the precipice of the hill. My body tumbled as I struggled to regain my senses, but then I felt a crack on the base of my skull, which was followed by a brief spike of pain. Then it disappeared—it was gone. All of it —the light, the pain, my life. It was all gone in an instant.

CHAPTER TWENTY-FIVE

The next time I woke, the sun hung low on the horizon, throwing its lazy last rays upon the Earth. I hadn't expected to see that because I thought that by now I would have died. Death was elusive, and this was most likely the devil's final trick. First, he would allow my human form to suffer the ultimate agony and despair before dragging me into his realm. I'd never before backed down from a challenge. So I pushed myself to my knees to start the agonizing walk once more .

"Please, have a seat, Daniel." The voice came somewhere off to my right - where the sun was setting.

My body tensed involuntarily, but I felt neither pain nor soreness. Where had the pain gone?

"Who's there?" I asked, shielding my eyes from the sun in an attempt to get a clearer view of him. Slowly, a human shape solidified in my field of vision.

"A friend," the voice said. "I'm building a fire if you are interested in helping."

It was a male voice that spoke in a calm and steady

manner. It seemed somehow familiar, like an old friend long forgotten.

"How did you find me?" I asked.

There was no answer from the stranger. As the sun was setting, I watched while he stacked bits of flammable brush and thick sticks onto the neat pile. As the sun finally dipped below the horizon, I could clearly see the man—not just his movements. He had brown hair, maybe longer than mine. He had a beard, and although it was not perfectly groomed, it was tidy in the way of men who spent their days outdoors. He wore what any outdoorsman man would wear—a sturdy pair of jeans and well-worn boots. He did not look up from where he was lighting the fire with a pack of wooden matches.

"Who are you?" I asked.

Again, he ignored me. *I have to be dreaming.* My body felt odd, like I was having an out-of-body experience. My mind was clear, but when I watched the stranger building his fire, I knew it had to be a dream. It was pretty close to what I imagined my dreams to be: strange and inexplicable, minus the darkness, of course. There was always so much darkness in my dreams.

"Let's not think about that now Daniel," the man said.

"Excuse me?"

"The darkness—let's not think about it. We just had a beautiful sunset; let's enjoy it."

The kindling crackled, and I watched as the twigs caught fire, doing their work to ignite the larger pieces of wood.

"Lighting and tending a fire has always been one of my favorite things to do. It never gets old," the man said, with the wonder of a child.

For some reason his words catapulted me back in time to my childhood, when I'd run away from home. I had yet another fight with my mother, so I ran; finally I stopped running. The younger me had a little black lighter that I had stolen from a convenience store. I stopped that evening to build a fire to stay warm during the frigid night.

At the sight of those first flames catching, a warmth spread throughout my entire body. Even though the night might have been cold, I no longer felt alone.

"I remember those days too," the man said, snapping me back to the present day. "That one was the first time you ran away. Do you remember why?"

I wanted to ask how he knew of such a personal event in my life. For a moment, I couldn't recall the reason myself.

The man answered for me, "You had asked your mother about your dad. She didn't want to tell you, so you screamed at her. You were only seven, and you did the only thing you could think of—you ran." He shook his head in wonder. "Even then you were searching. But how could you know the truth? You've always been so strong. And now you've discovered that strength isn't enough."

He offered no further explanation as he stirred the fire with a stick, tending to any sparks that flew out of the makeshift fire pit. Then it all made sense.

"I'm dead," I said.

The man chuckled. "No. You're not dead, Daniel. That won't happen for quite some time."

"Then I *must* be dreaming."

The man didn't respond, but he pulled a thin rubber band from around his wrist, tying his loose hair back in a ponytail. He still hadn't looked at me, which I found strange. I tried examining his face. For some reason, I couldn't make out his features. They were indiscernible; it wasn't like he was blurry or a ghost. If you asked me to describe him now, I'm not sure I could. All I knew was that his facial features and his body language projected absolute kindness. He exuded the confidence of a man so at home in his own skin that nothing could shake his confidence.

"She loves you, you know?" the man said.

"Who? My mother?" My mom had recently taken a turn for the worse. Years of abusing her body had segued into severe mental instability. Once, after the Corps, I'd visited her. Her appearance had left me so shaken that I vowed never to visit her again. I'd kept that promise.

"Yes, your mother loves you—in her own way," the man said. "But that's not who I was referring to just now."

Who was he talking about?

"Your friend. The one you call The Beast. She loves you."

I took a step back. Even if this was a dream, I'd never been confronted like this. It left me rattled. I expected any moment for the strange man to rise and pluck the life out of me. That's how my dreams usually went.

"We won't hurt you, Daniel," the man said, obviously reading my thoughts. "How do you feel right now?"

"Confused," I said honestly.

"That's good. Do you mind if I call to her?"

I almost said, "Call who?" but I knew who he was talking about, so I didn't say a word.

Still looking at the fire, the man spoke something in a foreign tongue. My body shivered from the sound. Then I caught the dark shadow to my side. I turned to see an impossibly large black panther padding towards the man.

The man kept tending the fire, but he took time to greet The Beast with his left hand. It lowered its head and then its body to the ground. With obvious affection, the man stroked the animal, and the cat's throaty grumble of acceptance shook me from the inside out. The Beast made itself comfortable next to the man. Had the man been standing, The Beast's head, while resting on the ground, would have easily reached the man's thigh. It was like no cat I'd ever seen before, with sleek muscles bulging and rippling under ebony fur.

I knew what it was, but I couldn't say it. I'd never truly seen it. I'd only felt its presence and known it was there deep inside me.

How could it be here now? Even in my dreams, The Beast had never emerged. It was always the primal half of my humanity. Then in unison, both the stranger and The Beast looked up at me. At first, there was no color there, just a void, like the endless eternity of life itself. It was as if I'd fallen into a hole that led to the other side of the universe. Then color returned and I saw both his eyes and The Beast's eyes. They were a vivid iridescent mixture of blues, greens, browns and yellows all combined and shaped into a magnificent master-piece by a skilled artisan. My breath caught.

"Beautiful, isn't she?" the man said smiling at me, scratching The Beast behind the ears.

"Why are you here?" I asked for the second time.

"I thought you might enjoy some company."

"I don't even know who you are."

"You know who I am. If you haven't figured it out by now, you soon will."

"But, this is impossible. That animal. That—"

"She is part of you, Daniel. You commanded her to protect you. She is now as much a part of you as your left hand or your right foot. She will serve you if you will serve her."

"But it's bad. It makes me do things that—"

"*She'd* prefer it if you call her 'she'," the man said, provoking a growl of assent from The Beast, "Not an *it*. She is not an *it*. Are you an *it*?" He took the massive head in his two hands, tossing it back and forth, playfully. The cat licked the man's hand, eliciting another laugh.

Then the stranger said, "You came here to die. I under-stand that, but it's not your time, Daniel. There's much left for you to do."

I almost asked how he could know what I had to do, but I knew it was fruitless. Despite the fact that The Beast was sitting across from me, the anger was still deep in my being. This strange dream, hallucination, or whatever I was experiencing had to end soon.

"I'll stay for as long as it takes," the man said. He continued to sit there as The Beast fell asleep, and the fire continued to crackle.

I contemplated my next move as the stranger waited patiently. *But what was it he was waiting for?*

CHAPTER TWENTY-SIX

At some point, lulled by the warmth and hypnotic glow of the fire and the stranger's calm demeanor, I felt a profound peace that I don't remember ever feeling before. No, that was wrong. I had felt peace before. Not all day—not every day—but snippets of it. Fire had always been central to that peaceful feeling. As he'd said, whenever I ran away, I hid in the woods and I lit a fire. Gazing into the flames was when I felt most at home. But what had the stranger said? He had been there? And that's exactly what it felt like. Like that fire somehow had taken the pain away, much like a soothing balm on burned skin. And then I knew the truth. It had nothing to do with the fire, but instead everything to do with the stranger.

"Were you really there?" I asked.

"I was always there, Daniel."

"Why didn't you say anything?"

"It wasn't time."

"But I needed you, and you weren't there. I was just a kid, and you didn't say anything."

"Just because I didn't say anything didn't mean that I

wasn't protecting you. Look back over your life, and tell me what you see."

I did as the stranger asked. All I could see was death, and that's what I told him.

"It's easy to be overwhelmed by death," he said. "Look deep into your heart. Can you tell me that you *didn't* do things for the right reasons? Haven't you looked for the good in people and often found it?"

"But all the things I've done—"

The stranger nodded thoughtfully. "Why do you do it - help all those people who are unable to help themselves?" he asked.

I didn't want to answer. I didn't want him to throw my words back at me, yet I answered despite my misgivings.

"Because it was, and is, the right thing to do," I said. "But why doesn't it feel that way now?"

"In every man and woman lives a seed of doubt. It's part of being human. But you've also been given the gift of joy. There is a part of you that understands how beautiful the world can be. Maybe you'll understand it better this way. Have you ever had a situation where your heart tells you to do one thing, but your head veers you in another direction?"

"Of course," I said.

"So, how do you choose whether to listen to your heart or head?"

"I don't know; I guess it depends on the situation."

"You're right, it does. But how do you, and I mean *you* specifically, Daniel Briggs, know the right path to choose?"

"Sometimes I don't," I said honestly.

"Yes. That honest admission is something you should never forget. It makes you different than most of humanity. You recognize your weaknesses, and yet you push on despite them. The world needs you, Daniel. But it needs the *whole* you that embraces both the doubt *and* the joy. The heart *and* the mind. You will not always know what to do, and that's part of your journey. Find your joy. Understand the gift you bring to the world. *They* need you Daniel. *I* need you."

I stared at the stranger, momentarily unable to comprehend his words. He said *they* needed me. He said *he* needed me. It was hard to wrap my mind around that responsibility. Once you cast your lot with the dregs of society, you're admitting that you have no worth. That's how I felt. I knew I had certain talents, but sometimes they felt more like hindrances than gifts.

But what if this man was telling the truth? What if there was more to life than what I had been living? What if—?

"What about her?" I asked, pointing to The Beast, who was now fast asleep next to the man.

The stranger smiled.

"She'll *always* be a part of you, Daniel. *She* is you, and *I* am you. You will come to know that."

The man stood, and he bent down to stroke The Beast's head one last time. He walked around the fire and stood before me. I held my breath in his presence.

"Relax," he said. "I won't bite, but I will always be here with you. No matter what happens, I am with you. If you need me, all you have to do is call." He reached down and placed a hand on my shoulder. Tears streamed down my face. I didn't want him to go. If this was a dream, I didn't want to wake up. Something about being in his presence made me feel full, alive and worthy.

"Show them who you really are, Daniel. Don't be afraid. Some will love you, and some will fear you. But understand this. Whether you never say another word in your life, it is through your actions that you will be judged. And before you ask, no, I will not judge you. I know you. But *they* will." He pointed out to the horizon, then turned back to the fire and motioned to the sleeping beast. "Take care of her, and in turn she will take care of you." He looked back to me and touched me first on my chest and then on my head. It was a last reminder to live my life using both my heart *and* my head. "Remember, Daniel. You *are* loved."

Without another word, he turned away from me and walked off into the darkness. I was left knowing my life had been irrevocably changed.

CHAPTER TWENTY-SEVEN

I don't remember either lying down or falling asleep. When I awoke, my limbs ached and my body begged for water. I opened my eyes slowly as my body let out an involuntary shiver. I expected to see a smoldering fire but there was none. The Beast wasn't lying there either. When I called to her, I felt her inside me. I sat up wearily, taking in my surroundings.

I'd somehow made it off the hill and was sitting in a ravine that had been washed out. How had I gotten there?

I rose slowly to my feet. The soreness and cramping in my legs screamed at me for relief. I took one deep breath after another. I was thirsty and in pain, but the weight of the burden that I had been carrying for so long felt noticeably lighter.

In that moment, for some unknown reason, I recalled a favorite line, "Get busy living or get busy dying." It was from one of my favorite movies, *The Shawshank Redemption*. I smiled at the recollection of Red, played by Morgan Freeman, and when his character made the life-altering decision which set him on the path to reunite with his old friend.

Something in me *had* changed. In the past, I had experienced moments of clarity when the fog had lifted, and I was able to see the world clearly. This new sensation was like that but many times over. I suddenly appreciated the fact that I was standing there, and I was filled with gratitude for all the second chances I had been granted. By all rights, I should be dead. I'd been cast into impossible situations—too many times to count. A sniper's bullet flown high. An enemy mortar round lobbed just off-target. A tiny ledge snagged at just the right moment. Each time I had escaped death's grasp. I must have looked so silly standing in the middle of the desert, grinning like a kid on Christmas morning. I was miles away from anyone and anywhere.

I won't say that everything changed with the revelation, but I would never return to my old ways. Something in me had inherently changed, and I hoped it would last until I'd had a chance to repay The Stranger's kindness.

Stepping out of the ravine, I knew that from then on, I would live my life with a whole heart. No longer would I live my life tethered by regret or burdened by worry. I held tight onto the revelation that I would not fail. I just had to choose to have faith in myself and hope in others. It would not be an easy journey, but when had I ever chosen the easy route?

My legs picked up speed, and I now walked with a fierce determination. It was reassuring that my always-present friend—The Stranger from the hill—would forever be walking alongside me in my journey. Given time, I would again find my purpose in life. I would find my way; I would find my family.

So there we were, Daniel and The Beast, walking on as one, forever linked. In those first steps together, I was filled with a renewed hope for the future, and a sense of inevitable glory for the good of mankind.

CHAPTER TWENTY-EIGHT

The old rancher cursed his shaking hands as he tried to sweep the front porch. The blowing desert wind sprinkled every inch of his property with a fine layer of dust.

"At least it isn't cancer," he said, smiling at his own joke while doing his best to sweep, despite the intermittent desert winds mocking his attempts. In a couple of hours, his maid would make her weekly trip, look at his handiwork, shake her head and then grab the broom to perform a thorough job.

When he was confident that he would receive no more than a lifted eyebrow from the housekeeper, he deposited the broom in the front coat closet and went to make his rounds. He liked to think of himself as a scientist at heart, and the ranch was an extension of his curiosity. He'd spent decades in the oil business, traveling around the world, touching down in some of the world's most inhospitable regions while looking for the valuable black gold. While his colleagues searched for better ways to find and exploit the reserves tucked away in the African hinterlands, sandy deserts of Saudi Arabia, or remote patches of Asia, the rancher imagined a day when life-giving water could be pumped through continental pipelines from huge desalinization plants along the coasts. Wouldn't it be miraculous to see barren regions converted into green pastures and well-irrigated farmland?

So, when he finally retired from the oil business, he purchased a thousand acres in the Nevada desert. His friends called him crazy, and his family called him worse. They speculated about the waste of his small fortune he'd spent a lifetime accumulating. But it was mornings like this that made all the gibes worth it.

He greeted his chickens and his handful of cattle. Then he checked on the stalks of corn, rows of wheat, and potted tomato plants. There were many new plants, courtesy of the research team from UNLV. Earlier in the year, he had been approached by a professor at the university. He had heard that the rancher was doing some independent research on the viability of certain plants in arid climates. A deal had been struck, and now the rancher was happy to host all who wanted to use his land to further both his as well as their dreams. They brought with them water lines and plants, and most cherished of all, they brought with them their curiosity.

His last stop was the stables. Two horses whinnied when he entered. "Good morning, ladies. I brought you a gift." He stuck his hand in his pocket and produced a mixture of dried apple and sugar cubes. "All right now, take your turn. Take your turn. No need to be rude," he said as one horse tried to push the other out of the way. "There you go," he soothed as the second female snagged her treat.

The rancher always marveled at the beauty of these creatures. What in their DNA had allowed humans to tame them? Riding one was one of the few things that calmed his shaking hands. He loved them for their therapeutic powers.

"I'll be back in a bit. I'll leave it up to the two of you to choose who I take out for a ride today." He patted each one on the rump, and then went on to finish his morning inspections.

With his check of the research water pumps complete, the rancher headed to the house, a simple dwelling with three bedrooms and an open floor plan. "Bacon and eggs sounds good today," he said to himself. "No. Why don't we kick that up a bit? *Toast*, bacon and eggs."

He grinned at his own words and took one last look at the rising sun before stepping inside. He paused, straining to see through the light. There was a shadow there, still wavy in the distance as the heat of the day worked up the desert haze. The rancher stood still, waiting to see if the figure would come closer. Closer it came.

Sometimes stray animals came on his property – a cow that had busted through a neighbor's fence or a horse that had thrown its owner and wandered onto his land. The animal was always thirsty, and the rancher was happy to help.

As the dark form came closer, he recognized the elongated gait of a person. "That's a long way to be out," he said to no one in particular. He grabbed a chair to sit on the front porch while he waited for the arrival of his uninvited guest.

The man strode onto his land, and the rancher was surprised to find it was a face he recognized. He rose from the chair, a bottle of water in his hand.

"Daniel?" he asked the long-haired man walking towards him. His entire body was covered in the same layer of dust he just swept off the front porch. Daniel raised a hand in greeting.

"To what do I owe the visit?" the rancher asked. Daniel didn't say a word but pointed to the bottle of water. "Sure, I'm sorry. Here you go." Daniel uncapped the bottle, nodded his thanks and then downed its meager contents. "There's more inside. Plenty more of course, and I was about to make some breakfast. Are you hungry?"

"Yes, please," Daniel said. His words made the rancher stop to take a good long look at the young man who the rancher had met with Tom and his buddies. There was something different about him. His skin bore the reddish hue of a day or more spent under the severe rays of the sun. But his eyes. It was his eyes. They looked clear and full as if the man had just emerged from a mountain spring.

"Come on, let's get out of this heat," the rancher said after a spell. Daniel removed his shoes prior to entering. He offered to take off his dirty clothes as well.

"No, why don't you just come inside? Have a seat. I'll get you some more water, and we'll get breakfast going."

Daniel simply nodded, and the rancher could have sworn there was a grin on the man's face and his eyes were sparkling. *Maybe from the heat?* It was obvious that he was dehydrated, but maybe the exposure had muddled his brain. The rancher had seen it happen to men before.

Daniel took a seat at the kitchen table. He downed three plastic bottles of water. The bacon sizzled in a cast iron skillet. The eggs were ready, sitting on a plate next to the kitchen sink. "It'll be a couple more minutes for the bacon if you'd like to start on the eggs now."

"I can wait," Daniel said as he grabbed a fourth bottle of water. While he was preparing breakfast, the rancher surmised the reason for Daniel's visit. Tom's father told him about Tom's accident. Now that he thought about it, he'd asked the rancher about the blond-haired man who was now sitting at his kitchen table. Maybe he was on the run. Maybe the rancher had just given refuge to a criminal.

He shook that thought away almost as quickly as it had come. Despite his appearance, Daniel seemed changed. He was not the same man the rancher had met mere days before. He tried to put his finger on the change, but he came up lacking.

The bacon finally cooked, he set the pieces on a plate covered with paper towels. He brought the food to the table. "I've got some toast too."

Daniel forked himself half of the eggs and a couple pieces of bacon and then went about slowly eating his meal. He seemed lost in thought and didn't say a word until he was finished with the food.

"Thank you," Daniel said.

"You looked like you needed it."

Daniel nodded.

"I don't mean to pry but what exactly are you doing way out here?"

"It's a long story."

"Well, I'm a pretty good listener and if there's anything I can do to help, you know I will."

"Did you hear about Tom?" Daniel asked.

"I did. His father called me."

Daniel didn't say anything. Instead he grabbed another bottle of water and sipped it slowly.

"Daniel, I don't mean to pry, but did you have something to do with what happened to Tom?" Daniel shook his head. "Then what are you doing way out here? You're a long way from town."

Daniel set down the water bottle and looked straight into the rancher's eyes. "I had to see an old friend."

For the rest of his life, the rancher would never encounter another feeling that enveloped him so completely as when Daniel said those words. It was as if every moment of truth had been laid on the table. Daniel had found something in the desert. He'd gone searching, and emerged with a treasure so hallowed that only one word could describe it: peace.

The rancher had found his own peace years ago, after losing his wife to a long battle with cancer. He had retreated, ostracizing himself from his friends and what was left of his family. They had had no children, and maybe that was a blessing because he had wreaked havoc on his own life.

But then on a lark, he had bought the land in Nevada, and everything had changed. He had a purpose again. Somewhere among those rows of corn and in that hay-strewn barn, he had found himself. What the young man sitting across from him now exuded was something inexplicable. He knew that with every fiber of his being. The rancher found himself drawn to that power, and he wanted to ask Daniel to stay even though, for some reason, he knew that the young man had to leave.

"Is there anything else I can get for you? Water, eggs, more bacon, maybe?"

"I'm fine. Thanks," Daniel said.

"Sure, of course. Then maybe a shower? I'm sure I can rustle up a clean set of clothes or wash yours."

"A shower would be great."

"Then it's settled. Why don't I clean up the kitchen? The shower's right through there." The rancher pointed down the hallway. "Second door on the left."

"There's one last thing," Daniel said.

"What's that?"

"I wanted to thank you for the other day, for what you said to me. I didn't understand what you meant at the time, but I just want you to know that I appreciate it."

The rancher didn't know what to say. He'd seen the pain in the young man's eyes. Even with the glory of killing so many coyotes and the adulation of Tom and his friends, Daniel had seemed drenched in sorrow. The rancher had said those words because he'd been in that place. He had felt the depths of despair when all hope seemed to evade him.

"I hope they helped," the rancher said picking up Daniel's plates and taking them to the kitchen sink. He had never been at a loss for words before, except at his wife's funeral. As

Daniel rose and headed to the bathroom, the rancher tried to clear his mind as he scrubbed away at the dishes. He tried to uncover the truth behind what he had just seen. *A man changed*, he thought. Something broken was now whole.

The rancher smiled, glad that he had been alive to witness such a life-affirming event.

CHAPTER TWENTY-NINE

Tom came to slowly, the swirling mass of his brain punctuated by the pain messages from all over his body. He couldn't remember at first why he felt such pain. *Why can't I open my eyes?* he thought, *Oh God, I'm blind!*

Gradually he remembered how to open his eyes, and when he did open them just a millimeter, he closed them just as quickly. *Too bright.* He did the same thing maybe a dozen times until finally his eyes could handle the light. His eyes finally fluttered open. He was on his back on something soft. When he moved his arm, he realized it was tethered to something. When he reached across with his other arm, he winced.

"Take it slow," came a voice.

"Who's there?" Tom asked. He still couldn't see clearly—it was just a mishmash of colors. He only saw blobs.

"It's Daniel."

Daniel? Who is Daniel? Tom thought hard, and then, like a form creeping out from the shadows, he remembered.

"Daniel," he said.

Tom blinked furiously to get a better view of his new friend. There he was, sitting right next to the bed, waiting for Tom to wake.

"How long have I been out?" Tom asked.

"A little over a day, I think. I just got here. Your dad went downstairs to get some food."

"My dad? Why is my dad here?"

"The doctor said you might have some short-term memory loss," Daniel explained. "You suffered a concussion, and your body is pretty beat up, but they say you'll heal."

"Concussion?" At the words, Tom felt the pain keenly. "I don't remember," but then he did. "One of them hit me on the head," he said, quickly. "I was trying to help Jay and Benji. They took us by surprise."

"Don't force it," Daniel said.

The memories returned now like watching a movie. Tom said, "We were going somewhere. I'm not sure where. Maybe I was taking Benji home, and they must have followed us. I didn't get a view of who they were, but—" Then the image disappeared, and Tom exhaled. "It was right there," he croaked. "Daniel, could you get me some water? I don't know if I've ever been this thirsty."

Daniel grabbed a cup of water from across the room and handed it to Tom. His lip was shaking as he drank with nearly a quarter of the liquid running down the front of his hospital gown. "Man, that's good," he said after drinking the whole cup. "Who knew water could taste *that* good. Could you get me some more, please?"

Daniel grabbed the cup, refilling it. As he did, Tom watched the Las Vegas newcomer. Tom could have sworn he noticed or saw something different in Daniel. But it could just be his addled brain playing tricks on him. When Tom first met him, Daniel had that look of an animal that had been caged for too long. It seemed he couldn't stay in one place for very long, always thinking about running. But now—

Daniel handed him the cup and Tom drank. Once finished, Tom said, "Hey, maybe we should get ahold of that cop. What was her name? Sandra something."

"Verelli," Daniel furnished.

"That's right, Sergeant Verelli."

"She's dead, Tom."

"Wait, what? How can she be dead?"

"I think the same people that attacked you got her."

The memories were coming back too fast now. Tom shut his eyes, trying to sift through them all. "Oh, God. What happened to Jay and Benji?"

"They haven't turned up yet," Daniel said, "But I'll find them. I promise."

Tom opened his eyes to regard Daniel. Yes, there was something different about him. He exuded a quiet confidence. What had caused this change?

"I need to get out of this bed. I'm going to help you," Tom said, reaching for the call button that rang the nurse's station.

"You need to stay here and rest," Daniel said, before Tom could press the button. "Besides, I think you'll be safer here."

"But you need help."

"I'll be fine. I'm used to doing this kind of thing. Trust me, okay? If I can help Jay and Benji, I will."

For some reason, Daniel's words quelled Tom's panic.

"Okay, but you have to keep me in the loop and tell me what's going on."

Daniel nodded. "First, why don't you tell me exactly what you remember? I'm sure you'll have to repeat it soon to the police, but I want to hear it, if that's okay."

"Sure, of course. Anything that will help."

"Okay, when you crashed your Jeep—"

"Aw, man, I crashed my Jeep?"

Daniel nodded. "I looked through your pockets while you were in the ambulance. I hope you don't mind, but I needed a clue, and you were out of it. I found a card, a pink one, from The Frisky Filly."

"The Frisky Filly?" Tom said. "Why would I have their card in my pocket?"

"The owner said she knows you."

"Well, I do—but—I mean, I haven't seen her since I helped them buy that land."

"You really have no idea why that card was in your pocket?"

"No, I swear. Daniel, you have to tell me what's going on."

Before Daniel had a chance to tell him, Tom's father came in carrying two white paper bags of food.

"Oh, my God, you're awake!" he said, setting the bags at the foot of the bed. He moved closer and took Tom's hand. "How do you feel?"

"Kind of crappy."

"Okay. Has the doctor been in? Have the nurses checked you out?"

"No, not yet. No, I was just talking to Daniel."

"Well, let me go get them."

"I'm fine, Dad."

"No, I need to go get them. They said as soon as you woke up they needed to check on you."

"He's right, Tom," Daniel said. "Here, just press the call button."

"No," Tom said firmly. "Dad, do you mind giving us a minute?"

His father hesitated, obviously not wanting to leave the room. It was touching, but not the time.

"Sure, son. I'll be right back." His father left reluctantly.

Tom looked at Daniel.

"You remembered something, didn't you?" Daniel said.

Tom nodded, even though the movement sent pain shooting up and down his spine.

"There was a Cadillac following us. I thought it was nothing, but—well—I'm pretty sure they were the people who attacked us. Dammit, I should have been more careful."

"You had no way of knowing what would happen," Daniel said. "All right. You get better, and I'll check in when I know more."

Daniel patted Tom on the arm. He left Tom thinking whoever this new Daniel was, he would fix everything. There was a renewed resoluteness surrounding Daniel, and there was a look of absolute certainty in his eyes.

CHAPTER THIRTY

Margaret Taylor had no more tears left to shed. Veronica remained sedated at the hospital. Margaret didn't want to call her friends. She had tried to call her ex-husband, but he hadn't picked up the phone. Not for the first time in her life, she cursed him. He was a good and decent man, but maybe that had been part of the problem. Going back to her teenage years, Margaret had a wild streak. Although her ex had provided her with every luxury she'd ever wanted, and still supported her financially, that wasn't what she needed. And now he wouldn't even pick up the damn phone.

For a brief moment, she considered having a drink. She was a social drinker, but she knew it was a slippery slope. Any emotions she was experiencing were only magnified by the addition of alcohol. For example, if she was angry, a couple of glasses of Chardonnay would put her on the warpath. That's not what her daughter needed now.

A policeman said they'd been attacked, and she'd seen the bruises on Veronica's body. The last time Margaret had seen

Nathaniel, he and Veronica were headed to the pool. Nathaniel had shown off the neon swim trunks that Daniel selected for him. He couldn't stop talking about Daniel. Margaret had the feeling that Daniel was behind the attack. In her mind, he had to be in some way.

Veronica had lived a tough life. She and Margaret hadn't always seen eye-to-eye on things, but she had to believe that Veronica was on the mend. Maybe Daniel, this vagabond, sought to take advantage of the situation. *But who would harm a child?*

Oh, that poor beautiful boy.

Margaret reached for the phone again, again dialing her ex's number. After six rings, it went to voicemail. "Call me dammit. Pick up the phone and call me!"

She slammed the receiver down. Maybe a drink was exactly what she needed to calm down. She was about to get up and head to the mini-bar when there was knock at the door. She'd forgotten to put the "Do Not Disturb" tag on the doorknob.

"We're good, thank you," Margaret said in the sweetest voice she could muster. There was no need to be rude to the housecleaning staff.

"Ms. Taylor, it's Daniel."

Margaret froze. She should call the police. They'd been looking for the young man. They had related a policewoman had been killed in the line of duty, and Daniel was wanted for questioning.

No. If she turned him over to the police right now, she wouldn't get answers to her questions until they were done with him. Instead of doing the smart thing, and her civic duty, she stormed to the door, swinging it open.

"What did you do to Nathaniel?" she hissed.

Daniel didn't back away from her. Rather, he stood his ground and looked her straight in the eye.

"I didn't, and I wouldn't, hurt Nathaniel. Can I come in?"

Margaret wanted to lash out at Daniel. She wanted to kick and scream, accuse him of murder. As she looked at the young man, she found she couldn't. There was something about his demeanor—actually something in his eyes. It was the way he looked at her. Although every cell in her body wanted to believe he was guilty, she couldn't rail against him.

In that moment, she knew he was innocent.

"I'll leave," Daniel said.

The southern sensibilities of her prim and proper mother made an appearance; Margaret stepped aside.

"No, please. Come in."

Daniel nodded and stepped inside, careful to give Margaret her space. She closed the door, following him into the suite.

"I'm sorry I said that."

"There's no need, Ms. Taylor."

They stood there for a long while as Margaret waited for Daniel to speak, but he didn't. And then the dam broke and the tears that she thought had dried up began again streaming down her face. "That poor little boy. That beautiful little boy," she sobbed.

He stepped to her and held her as she cried. He didn't say a word. Margaret didn't know how long she cried. After chastising herself for losing her composure—especially in front of a stranger—she found herself grateful she was no longer alone.

"The police are looking for you," she blurted, not in an accusatory manner but more as a warning.

"I know," he said.

"Maybe you should go. They said they'd be by to pick me up and take me back to the hospital. I just had to gather some things and—"

"I know. They told me."

"The police?"

"No, one of the nurses. I went to see Veronica, but she was still sleeping." Another awkward silence followed. "Ms. Taylor, I hope it's all right, but I need to ask you some questions."

"But I don't know anything." Margaret couldn't understand why she was even considering speaking to this man. She believed in the law. She believed in civic duty and the police, provided to protect citizens. "I told the police everything I know, but if you think it would help," she heard herself saying.

"Sometimes the smallest detail helps most," he said.

"Well then, I want to help," Margaret said quickly.

"What happened after I left, after Veronica and I went to buy the bathing suits?"

Margaret didn't even have to think about it. She had replayed it over in her mind since getting the call about Nathaniel.

"They got dressed and left. Nathaniel wanted to jump on the water slide. Oh, God."

The tears returned again, this time without the sobs. She imagined the little boy in peals of laughter as he slid down into the pool landing in his mother's arms.

"How long after that did you hear from the hospital?"

"It wasn't the hospital; the police called me," Margaret corrected. "I'm not sure how long it was from the time they left to when I received the call. I'm embarrassed to say I had a glass of champagne – maybe two, after which I decided to take a nap. The call awakened me. And to be honest, I really thought it was a joke. Veronica and Nathaniel were supposed to be down at the pool, so how did they end up at the hospital?"

"And then what happened?"

"Well, I went down to the curb and caught a cab to the hospital. Veronica was a mess, so they had to sedate her. They made me identify Nathaniel's body. Oh, God. They had to wipe the blood from his face. It was all over him. At first I really thought it was that face paint the kids use on Halloween. That's what it looked like."

"I'm very sorry," Daniel said. "And I'm sorry I have to ask, but did anybody else come by? Did Veronica have any visitors?"

"No, no. It was just us." Then she paused. "Other than you, the only strange thing to have happened was the problem with the phone."

"The phone?"

Margaret pointed to the elegant contraption sitting on the coffee table. "The manager said he'd send somebody up to take a look at it."

"What was wrong with the phone?"

"It would ring, but when I picked it up, nobody was there."

Daniel thought about that for a moment and then asked, "Did Veronica ever pick up the phone?"

"Maybe once, I'm not sure. Why?"

"It could be nothing," Daniel said. "You're right. The manager should take a look at it. I'll remind him on my way out."

"Wait, you're going?"

"Don't worry, I'll see you at the hospital."

Margaret didn't want him to leave. For some reason, he was a calmness in the roiling seas.

"I can come with you. We can share a cab," Margaret suggested.

But Daniel shook his head, "This is something I need to do alone, but I promise we'll talk soon."

Daniel gave her a final nod of understanding, and upon his departure, left Margaret Taylor thinking that whoever had just been in the room was a completely different man than the one she'd met mere days ago.

CHAPTER THIRTY-ONE

Lieutenant Frank Salazar looked up in annoyance when someone dared to rap on his window. He'd told them: "No distractions."

A twenty-year veteran of the Las Vegas beat, Salazar was what Hollywood painted a cop to look like. He had a stubbly chin. His rough edges included a bark just as nasty as his bite.

"What?!"

The desk sergeant opened the door without a hint of contrition on his face. "Hey, Lieutenant. The guy they think killed Verelli just surrendered."

"Where?"

"Here, boss. He's out front."

Salazar was under the microscope by the mayor and the governor. A police officer had been killed—a female cop, no less. It looked like a set up. To make matters worse, Sergeant Sandra Verelli and Lieutenant Frank Salazar had been good friends. In fact, she was possibly the only friend Salazar had. He'd downed half a bottle of tequila the night before in her honor, and he was still feeling the effects.

"Put him in room three, and post a guard, damn it."

"Yes, sir," the desk sergeant said, a beat too slow.

"I said move!"

The man's pace increased, just perceptibly.

"Fucking young cops," Salazar murmured. If it were up to him, he would strip the department clean, and replace them with Verelli clones. She'd been good—very good. Not only could she handle politicians *and* the media, but she had been the best investigator Salazar had ever known. That had gone a long way toward convincing the one-time chauvinist that women really did know how to be cops.

Salazar's first thought as he went to meet the young punk was to go in swinging, literally, if he had to.

The coroner was taking his sweet time examining Verelli's body. Salazar had already returned to the scene. Her weapon had still been holstered. The back door of the cruiser was open. The cuffs were on the backseat. None of it made any sense. There was no way a cuffed prisoner could have done that. Even Harry Houdini himself wasn't good enough to pull one over on Sandra Verelli.

No, something else was going on, and he wasn't going to leave that interrogation room until he came out with answers. Then the image of his dead friend reminded him to be cautious in his questioning, much the way she had been. She busted more crooks with a few neatly placed words than a 400-pound cop could get throwing jabs.

When Salazar entered the holding room, he was all business. He'd even put on his sport coat, and he had a folder tucked neatly under one arm. The blond-haired boy looked up at him when he entered the room. He displayed no fear, just expectation of the forthcoming questions.

Salazar met his gaze for a moment and sat down. He set the folder on the battered metal desk which he opened slowly, arranging its contents in a neat row. He wanted nothing more than to jump across the table and break the young man's nose. Salazar was proud of the fact that, in the line of duty, he'd broken every knuckle in both hands. When a suspect swung at an officer, you had the constitutional right to swing back. And Lt. Frank Salazar knew how to swing back.

But he tempered his needs with what the investigation required. Salazar read the man his rights. He then asked the dreaded question, "Would you like the presence of an attorney? I could call one if you'd like."

The young man shook his head, "I don't mind talking to you."

"Okay, state your name for the record."

"Daniel Briggs."

"And, Mr. Briggs, you understand that you are currently wanted on suspicion for the murder of Sergeant Sandra Verelli?"

"I do."

"And you understand any answers you give me today could incriminate you in any legal proceedings?"

"I do."

Good, Salazar thought. He loved it when these idiots came in thinking there was no way the police could prove their guilt. When they waived the right to an attorney, it was game on, and Salazar had been in this rodeo for a long time. He tried to quiet the part of him that was unnerved by this man's ease. This Briggs character was as cool as they came. Maybe he was hopped up on something. There was no way he could make a move from where he sat. After all, he was shackled.

But something in the man's calm demeanor gave Salazar the briefest of pauses. Salazar's unease urged him to proceed carefully with the questioning.

"You were apprehended in the vicinity of The Frisky Filly two days ago, correct?"

"Yes, sir."

"And our records show that you were in the process of trying to get away when you were arrested."

"No, sir," Briggs said, "I turned myself in, just like I have today."

The first lie, Salazar thought. "Mr. Briggs, it says right here," Salazar tapped his finger on the piece of paper, "my officers had to use force to put you in the police cruiser."

"Define what you mean by force, sir."

Salazar was about to snap back and tell the guy it wasn't his job to define words. But he didn't.

"The arresting officer, who by default was someone other than Sergeant Verelli, says you were put on the ground, hand-cuffed, and placed in the police vehicle."

"Yes, sir. That's what happened."

"Are you telling me you didn't have to be physically restrained? That sounds like the definition of force to me," Salazar said smugly.

"No, sir. It did happen just the way you read it. My hands were up. They told me to lie on the ground. I complied with their request. The cuffs were placed on my wrists, and I was helped up. We walked to the police cruiser, and I was helped into the vehicle."

There was really no point in pressing Briggs on a small detail, but Salazar would still chew the officer's ass who'd been a bit too liberal with the description of the scene. In Salazar's mind, writing "forcibly" meant there had been an altercation or scuffle. The sprinkling of other descriptive terms equally rankled Salazar. Either the cop had become overzealous, or he wanted to inflate his own role in Briggs's arrest. Salazar filed that away for his next daily ass-chewing session.

"So you got in the back of the cruiser, and Sergeant Verelli was on her way to bring you back to the station herself. Is that correct?"

"Yes, sir," Briggs answered.

"And what did you talk about on the way here?"

"I didn't talk."

"What do you mean you didn't talk?"

"I was pretty upset."

"Ah, upset that you were arrested?"

"No, sir. I was upset about Nathaniel, the boy whose murder Sergeant Verelli said I was under arrest for."

Salazar had forgotten about that important detail, but he played it off. It would be a hell of a day if he could solve two murders in the span of one questioning.

"So, you were on your way to this station, and somehow you convinced Sergeant Verelli to stop. What did you tell her —you had to take a leak?"

"No, sir."

Salazar waited for further details, but none came.

"Well then what was it? How did you get her to stop in the middle of nowhere and let you out?"

"She stopped. I didn't say a thing."

Salazar stared at the man. "You realize how much sense that makes, right? Nobody in their right mind is going to believe that a good cop like Sandra Verelli would make such a bonehead move."

"I'm telling you what happened," Briggs said. And for the first time Salazar saw a force of will in the man's face. "I came here to help. Don't believe me if you want, but I'm telling you the truth."

"And why should I believe you, Mr. Briggs? You're wanted in two—yeah, that's right —two murder investigations. Tell me why in the hell I should listen to you."

"Because you're a tough cop, but you're a good cop," Briggs said without hesitation. "I can see that you respected Sergeant Verelli. I liked Sergeant Verelli. Any decent person knows that if a kid is murdered there are some bad people behind it. You want to solve those murders, and so do I. That's why I came to the station, and that's why I'm telling you the truth."

Salazar was not a man who lost his ability to speak, but as he stared at Briggs something deep inside him said that if he didn't listen carefully, bad things would happen. This was one of Lieutenant Frank Salazar's pivotal moments. It was the type that defines the rest of your life.

"Okay," he said, "tell me what happened next."

"Like I said, I was pretty upset," Daniel explained. "It took me probably a minute to realize that Sergeant Verelli was trying to get me out of the car. She said she needed to talk."

Salazar almost interrupted to check the validity of the story. *Why wouldn't Verelli have brought Briggs here to question him?* But he kept his mouth shut and listened.

"She got me out of the car and slapped me," Briggs said with a smile. If any other person had been sitting in front of him, Salazar would have thought that this was when the other shoe dropped—when a civilian brought a complaint against a dead police officer. But that's not what Briggs did.

"I snapped back to reality," Briggs continued, "and she said that she knew I hadn't killed Nathaniel. She thought something else was going on. She had her suspicions, and I'm pretty sure she wanted my help to figure it out. "

"Hey, look," Salazar said. "Verelli was a good cop. Why would she ask for *your* help?"

"I think you just answered your own question," Briggs said. "She was a good cop. She knew that she needed help. I was willing to give it, but we never got that far. About the shot that took her life—I don't think it was a long shot. It was made from a distance of around 200 yards."

"How could you know that?"

"I just know," Briggs said. "I have experience. I've had

some time to think about it, and the only thing I can figure is that someone was following us. They'd probably tailed Sergeant Verelli for a while. I don't know. Maybe they'd suspected we'd stop, or maybe it was prearranged. I'll never know. So what happened? Sergeant Verelli fell, and I ran."

"Hold on. You ran. If you're such a hero, why didn't you call for back up?" Salazar had read the entire report three times. Verelli's weapon was still on her person. There was a shotgun inside the cruiser as well as a functioning radio.

"I was outgunned," Briggs said, "and I didn't want to die. Isn't that reason enough?"

Salazar knew he was right. If what Briggs was saying was true, and whoever had taken the shot was only 200 yards away, Briggs would have been a sitting duck.

"All right, let's assume that what you say is true. Someone, some anonymous sniper 200 yards away takes out one of my officers, and you just run away? You know how that's going to look to the court, right?"

"Sure, it'll look like a set up," Briggs said. "But I'm telling you I had nothing to do with it."

Salazar knew he was on a slippery slope. Maybe it'd be best to hand this Briggs character off to the lawyers. Let them have a field day. Once all the details were in from the crime scene, they would have a better idea of what really happened. But the veteran police officer couldn't shake the feeling that what Briggs said was the exact truth.

"So, let's say we go along with this assumption that there's a pretty good lone gunman out there. Why do you think they let you go?"

"I've been thinking about that," Briggs said, "and all I can conclude is that they still need me for something they have planned."

"And what do you think that is?"

Briggs shook his head, "I don't know yet."

"Okay, then we're at a standstill until the coroner's report comes back, and my team has had time to digest the scene. You're spending tonight in jail."

"That's not going to happen," Briggs said confidently.

"Oh? And why not?"

"Because you're going to let me go."

Salazar actually laughed. "And why would I want to do that?"

"Because you want to find out who killed Sandra Verelli."

"And how will releasing you from police custody help me find her killer?" Salazar asked, tightlipped.

"Because I'm going to find that person for you, and then I'm going to kill that person."

CHAPTER THIRTY-TWO

Lieutenant Salazar grinned. *I've got you now, you smug bastard.* "Thank you for your admission, Mr. Briggs." Salazar rolled up a sleeve. "I'll have one of my officers along shortly to escort you to the finest jail cell the Las Vegas PD has to offer."

"I know what you're thinking," Briggs said.

This should be good, Salazar thought. "The only thing *you* should be thinking right now is how quickly they're going to put you on death row."

"That's actually not what I was going to say. You're thinking that it was stupid to say that I was going to kill someone."

Salazar glanced at his watch and sighed. "Okay, I've got a couple minutes. Why don't you go on and tell me how you can read my mind? And yes, what you just said was the first thing I thought. You must be a genius."

"But you're wrong. I didn't say I *wanted* to kill them. I said I'm *going* to kill them.

"You seem to think there's a distinction between the two.

Under the law, you are a murderer either way," Salazar said, already boring of the conversation.

"The difference is, I won't have a choice. If you had asked me three days ago, I would've said, "Yes, I want to kill that person." But now, I know that I won't be given a choice."

Salazar exhaled. "Everyone has a choice, Mr. Briggs. When you're standing in front of a judge, he won't have sympathy for your 'I didn't have a choice' routine."

"It'll never come to that," Briggs said.

These punks are all the same, Salazar thought. *They get busted, and they still can't believe that they're going to spend the rest of their lives in jail.*

For Briggs, a lethal injection was the likely outcome. And so, because he had nothing better to do for the next five minutes, Salazar indulged him. "And why won't you be standing in front of the judge? How do you know that with absolute certainty?"

That's when Briggs smiled and said, "I have faith."

The first snort of a belly laugh came out as the interrogation room door flung open.

"Hey, Lieutenant, can I speak with you?"

Salazar played it off, but deep down, the interruption was one more black mark on his department. He moved to the doorway.

"What is it?"

"The woman in the hospital."

"*What* woman in the hospital?"

The officer looked down at the sheet of paper in his hand. "Ms. Taylor—Veronica Taylor."

Salazar's eyebrows shot up. "Is she dead?"

"What? No, sir. She recanted her statement. She's saying this guy *didn't* kill her son."

Salazar's head turned ever so slowly back to Briggs, and then back to his police officer.

"Are you going to let him go, Lieutenant?"

"No, I'm *not* going to let him go. He's a killer. He just admitted it to me." Salazar was sure of that now. Briggs's admission to kill the perpetrator was just the icing on the cake with a blood-red cherry on top. "I'll read the full report when I get done," Salazar said.

The officer lingered as if there might be a show, so Salazar glared at him. He got the point, finally.

"So, she's awake now," Briggs said once the door had closed. Salazar didn't answer. "Things are moving faster," Briggs continued.

"You know what," Salazar said. His palms were on the table now, his body towering over Briggs. "I'm getting a little tired of your smug attitude. Twenty years ago, I'd put you in a cell full of bruisers. I'll bet more than one of them wouldn't take kindly to finding out that you killed a little boy. But now I have to be careful and protect your rights," Salazar said with a sneer. "But, that's okay. I've learned to be a patient man. I know that in the end, you'll get your due, one way or another. It'll come."

Briggs didn't flinch, and he didn't look away. He was a tough case all right. Salazar would enjoy seeing him burn. But as soon as he moved to call for assistance in having Briggs escorted away, the door swung open—again. The same officer's face appeared. This time he was wide-eyed and flushed.

"What is it?" Salazar growled.

"Sir, you've got a phone call."

"Take a message. Tell them I'll call them back."

"No, sir. You need to take this."

"If it's not God on that phone, so help me—"

"It's the governor, Lieutenant."

The governor? Why's the governor calling me? He'd only met the old man once, when the governor had shown up with his entourage of foreign investors. They had expected royal treatment, and Salazar's officers had played babysitters. The moneymen had wined, dined, and gambled through Las Vegas.

"I'll be with him in a moment," Salazar said quickly, trying to hide his unease. Then, he glanced back at Briggs and thought he saw something there. Recognition maybe, or was it... No, now he was just seeing things. *Take a deep breath, Frank. You turned over a new leaf, remember?* He took a deep breath. "I'm not done with you," he said to Briggs, and then he stomped out of the room.

The bullpen was quiet when he entered. Everyone was staring—at him. He didn't like it. "Get back to work," he barked. Then, he went into his office and closed the door. There was a single, blinking light that meant somebody was on hold. He picked up the phone and pressed the lit button.

"Lieutenant Salazar," he said.

"Ah, Lieutenant. So, nice of you to take my call," the governor said.

"Yes, sir, I'm sorry to have kept you waiting."

"You are in the middle of an investigation, I understand."

"Yes sir. Is there something I can help you with, Governor?"

"Ah, yes. You have a prisoner by the name of Daniel Briggs, is that correct?"

Salazar's heart started galloping. "You know I'm not at liberty to say."

"Oh, come on, Lieutenant." The kind politician was gone, replaced by someone used to getting his way. "In no less than ten minutes I've received phone calls from one senator and four congressmen. Would you like to know what those calls were about?"

"Yes, sir," Salazar said, trying to sound confident.

"They would like to know why we have a Marine—a

Marine hero, I might add—in our custody without any formal charges."

"Sir, I can—"

"No. Lieutenant, *you* listen. I don't appreciate getting calls from senators and congressman. Further, I don't like being informed the Las Vegas Police Department has arrested an innocent Marine and future Medal of Honor recipient."

"Medal of Honor?"

"Yes, Lieutenant. You do know what the Medal of Honor is, right?"

The question was like a slap in the face. Of course he knew what the Medal of Honor was, but all he could get out was, "Yes, sir."

"Oh, good. At least we're on the same page with that one. Now, here's what's going to happen, Lieutenant. I've already confirmed that all the charges have been dropped."

"Sir, I don't—"

"I said *listen*, Lieutenant. Now that all charges have been dropped against Mr. Briggs, you will release him."

"But, sir, we still have an investigation to—"

"Would you like me to call the president? Would you like me to tell him that Lieutenant Frank Salazar went against his wishes, and despite having any credible source you held a bona fide American hero in police custody?

Salazar was finally able to regain his wits. "Sir, Mr. Briggs is suspected of killing one of my officers. You met her, Sergeant Sandra Verelli."

"Yes, I remember Sergeant Verelli," the governor said, "She was a very capable woman. It's a shame and a loss to the department. According to the coroner's report as well as your own department's investigation, the case against the Marine is closed. There is no way Mr. Briggs could have shot Sergeant Verelli with a hi-caliber rifle from two feet away. I believe the estimate was a two hundred yard shot."

Salazar was shocked that the governor had those details at hand. "Yes sir, but I —"

"Let him go, *now*," the governor said. Then his voice changed, "I'm not telling you that you shouldn't keep an eye on him, Lieutenant. Until he commits a crime that you can verify, he is not to be in Las Vegas PD custody. Is that understood?"

"Yes, sir," Salazar said.

"Good, I'll let the people in Washington know. And Frank—"

"Yes, sir?"

"I look forward to seeing you again. How about the next time I'm in town, I treat you to dinner?" There was the sound of a click, indicating the conversation with the governor was over.

Salazar just sat there drowning in shock for a long while. He attempted to digest the Briggs case as well as his twenty-plus years as a cop. He'd seen some strange things: He'd seen a bullet enter a man's torso and exit through his foot. He'd witnessed politicians caught up in a cross-dressing sex ring. But nothing could've prepared him for this situation involving Daniel Briggs.

Daniel Briggs's earlier prediction had come true. It was not in a, "Oh, he was right," manner, but rather two minutes later, reality was being swept aside.

Lieutenant Frank Salazar was stuck. He rose to his feet and set his jaw. Then he went about doing as he had been ordered - procuring the release of Daniel Briggs.

CHAPTER THIRTY-THREE

The phone conversation began absent a greeting. The owners of the two garbled voices were already well acquainted.

"They just released him."

"Good. Let's move to the next phase."

"How long before you can join me?"

"It'll be soon now."

"What about the cops?"

"They don't have a clue. They still think he did it."

"Do you think it was smart to involve them?"

"It's more fun this way, and you know it. Now stop talking about what could have been. Any lingering doubts about the kid?"

A long pause ensued. "No. No doubts."

"Good. Because he was the key, and you know it. He provided the perfect bait and switch."

"I know. It just wasn't easy."

"It'll all be over soon. Maybe afterward we'll take a little vacation."

"Okay."

"I almost forgot. Good call tipping off the Feds."

"Yeah."

"Okay, then. It won't be long now. Can't you feel it?"

"I can."

"Good. Stay the course. It'll all be over soon."

"I know."

CHAPTER THIRTY-FOUR

The plainclothes detective reached for the radio. "He just went into the hospital room, Lieutenant."

Salazar's voice crackled. "Roger. Don't follow him in. Stay where you're at."

"Yes, sir."

"Keep me posted."

"Roger. Out."

———

"I'M SORRY, sir. I can only allow family to visit her."

"He's with me. Thank you," came a voice from behind him. Margaret Taylor gave a short wave to Daniel, and the nurse let him pass.

"I was getting worried about you."

"I had a stop to make."

"Is everything okay?" Margaret asked.

"Just fine. How's Veronica doing?"

"She's better. At least she's lucid now. But—well—she did lose her child."

Daniel nodded. "Can I see her? I promise I won't upset her."

Margaret hesitated. She had told him the truth. Veronica was better, but only in comparison to her earlier screaming hysterics. "I would caution against saying too much. She doesn't want to talk," Margaret warned.

"I understand," Daniel said. "Here, I picked you up some coffee."

Margaret hadn't even noticed the cardboard holder in his hands.

"Oh, thank you." She took the insulated coffee cup and led the way.

Veronica was in the same position as when her step-mother had left her. She was staring listlessly out the window.

"Honey, Daniel's here to see you."

When Veronica's head turned, her eyes were bloodshot and swollen. She seemed to be focusing on multiple forms coming into the room. "Daniel?" she asked.

"It's me," Daniel said, stepping up to the bed. Veronica reached out her hand which Daniel took.

"I'm so sorry about what I said to the police. I was confused, and your name came out first. I shouldn't have said that. I hope I didn't get you into any trouble."

Veronica began crying again.

"It's taken care of," Daniel said. "We're more worried about you right now."

Veronica turned back to face the window although she remained holding Daniel's hand.

"Have you ever lost anyone, Daniel? Someone close?" she asked.

"I have."

"When will this feeling of emptiness go away?"

"It never really does."

Veronica snatched her hand back. She shook her head

from side to side. Margaret thought she would have to call the nurse again to have her stepdaughter sedated. Her finger was poised above the call button.

"I don't know what happened. One minute, we were having fun at the pool and the next—Oh, God—" Veronica covered her face with her hands and sobbed. To his credit, Daniel just waited for the emotion to play itself out. When Veronica was done, she looked up at him with her eyes blazing. "I want you to find them, Daniel. I want you to find them for me, and for Nathaniel."

Daniel nodded. Margaret's throat tightened. What had just passed between the two of them? Whatever it was, she didn't like it. The police had told them that they had some leads. The police could handle it. Why was Daniel playing into Veronica's whims like that? His indiscretion made her want to push him out the door and instruct him to never return.

Daniel broke Margaret's concentration by asking "Did you get ahold of your ex-husband yet?"

"What? No. He's still not answering his phone."

"Maybe you should have the police run by his house, just in case."

Margaret had been too distraught to even consider that option.

"Do you think something's happened to him?"

"It could be nothing," Daniel said, still staring at Veronica.

"Okay, I'll call the police as soon as you leave," Margaret said, hoping that time would be soon. There was no need to get Veronica riled up again.

Daniel reached out and touched Veronica lightly on the arm. "We'll get this whole thing figured out. I promise."

Veronica nodded. She was already covering her face with

her hands again, muffling her sobs and trying to conceal her pain.

Margaret followed Daniel out the door.

"You may want to see if they can keep her sedated," Daniel suggested.

"I'll try," Margaret said noncommittally. "With her history of drug abuse, Veronica is hesitant. She's afraid she will become dependent on drugs again."

Daniel nodded. "You should be safe here, but just make sure you keep an eye on her."

He made it sound like an army of black-clad men were preparing to storm the hospital. It made Margaret shiver.

"Please tell me you're helping the police."

"Something like that," Daniel said. "But like I said, stay here. The police have the place surrounded. You see that guy in the waiting room—the one with the brown shirt?"

Margaret nodded.

"He's a plainclothes cop. Go to him first should anything happen."

Margaret was about to ask how Daniel knew the man was a police officer providing protective detail. But Daniel was already walking away.

"Daniel!" Margaret called out.

He turned his head. "Don't worry, I'll stay out of trouble."

But there was something in his eyes. It wasn't quite a glimmer of amusement, but something close to it. He turned and continued down the hallway.

Margaret went back to the room and resumed the vigil over her grieving stepdaughter. Then she remembered what Daniel had said. She quietly left the room. It took some time, but she was finally able to reach the West Los Angeles police. Their department served the Pacific Palisades area. After a brief conversation, the officer on the line promised someone would stop by her ex-husband's house to check on things.

They would call once they knew more, but the officer on the line did tell her that this sort of thing happened all the time.

Margaret wasn't sure if she should feel worry or relief after hanging up. She did know that she was ready for this nightmare to be over.

CHAPTER THIRTY-FIVE

"Lieutenant, he just left the hospital in a cab."

"Which way is he going?" Salazar asked.

"I'll tail him, and let you know."

Five minutes later, the officer called in. "Lieutenant, he's headed out of town. Do you still want me to follow him?"

"Of course I do. What direction is he heading?"

"Looks like he might be going back to The Frisky Filly."

Salazar said, "I'm sure he knows that you're following him."

"I've been careful, Lieutenant. He hasn't seen me."

"He's seen you; trust me. I don't think he'll start any trouble. But just in case, stay back a safe distance."

The officer rolled his eyes, glad his Lieutenant couldn't see the eyeroll. *This ain't my first rodeo, Grandpa*, he thought. "Roger that," he said into the radio. Then he drove on, following the taxi cab that had a David Copperfield ad on the roof.

"YES. Thank you very much, Lieutenant. I'll be careful."

The owner of The Frisky Filly hung up the phone. She wondered if she'd been wrong in refusing a police presence at her establishment. But then again, the impromptu search days before had already put them behind for the month. Word leaked out quickly. She could ill afford to have the police snooping around. There was no quicker way to lose potential customers than for them to see a police cruiser sitting outside her den of pleasure.

She stood up from her desk and padded down the hallway. She'd beefed up her security detail after the incident with Briggs. She wasn't going to be caught flat-footed again. She met him at the front door, accompanied by six armed bodyguards. Her detail included the two with the well-earned bruises on their faces.

Daniel emerged from the cab and walked straight to her. The two security guards caught by surprise before, moved to intercept him. She waved them away.

"You knew I was coming," Daniel said.

"A little birdie told me," the owner said with a sly grin.

"Would you like to talk here or inside?" Daniel asked.

"I thought we'd take a walk."

Daniel nodded. She motioned her bodyguards to stay a respectable distance behind. It was still hot, but the sun had already dipped beyond the hills. They wound their way along the dirt bike trail constructed by the previous property owner.

Once they were far from The Frisky Filly, she said, "I understand you met Lieutenant Salazar."

"I did."

"And what did you think of him?" The owner was genuinely interested.

"He's a good cop."

The owner grunted. "Sometimes I feel like the man has made it his mission to keep me miserable."

Daniel ignored the comment and asked, "I need to know how you met Veronica's father."

"I've never met him."

"Then how did he know to call you?"

"He called me out of the blue. He's never spent time here before. At least not that I'm aware of," she said honestly.

"Did the police ask you about him?"

"They know better than to dig into my business dealings. I've got the best lawyers in Vegas on retainer—I have to. Besides, no crime was committed on my land."

"And what about Veronica? What did they ask you about her?"

"The same thing you just asked me about her father. Had I met her, and could I give them a brief description. So, I did. I told them the truth. I'd never really met her. I'd seen pictures and she was pretty enough."

"And what about Nathaniel? Did they ask you about him?"

"They did. They wanted to know if I'd seen the boy, and of course I never had, so that was that."

"And what did they ask you about me?"

The owner chuckled, "Oh, they wanted to know *everything*. They wanted to know what we had talked about. They asked what services you'd had while you'd been here. You know, the usual questions."

"And what did you tell them?"

"I told them that we talked, and that you weren't the right fit to be part of my illustrious clientele."

"Why didn't you tell them the truth?"

"Selfish reasons. If they think that I'm somehow connected with you, they'll hang around more. If they hang around more, I lose money. So, it's fair to say, you were some random guy who wasn't happy with the way we offered to get his rocks off."

Daniel didn't seem offended and just nodded as they walked. "How bad has business been?"

The owner looked surprised at the question. "What do you mean?"

Daniel looked at her, "You told me last time that ever since agreeing to hire Veronica things had gone wrong"

The owner hesitated, "I was saying that generally. It's been more of a headache than anything else."

They kept walking. "And what about your two employees? The ones found in the motel? Did you tell Salazar about them?"

"He never asked."

"Why do you think that is?" Daniel asked.

"Probably because we never filed a missing person claim. That was on them. Besides we don't even know if it was them."

"It was them." Daniel said

The finality of the comment made the owner swallow hard. "Why did you come here?" she asked when she finally caught her breath.

"I wanted to warn you. I can also help, if you will accept it."

"You help me? Now honey, that's not the way it works around here."

"I know that prostitution is not your only business," he said.

"Just what are you implying?"

"I'm not implying anything. I'm stating the facts. This place is too expensive for your average Joe. So, that means high-end clientele, and that type of clientele represents another opportunity."

"I don't know what you're talking about."

"I don't care what you do in this place. It's none of my business, but what you're doing will get you killed."

The way he said it, so matter-of-factly gave the owner pause. "When did you figure it out?"

"I had a hunch, and you just confirmed it."

The owner nodded, "It's not drugs, if that what you're thinking."

"I assumed blackmail—extortion."

That actually made the owner laugh. "I'm not *that* old-fashioned. It comes down to a single word—information. I keep my clients happy. In various ways, in turn, they keep me happy. The information I glean is much more lucrative than having twenty girls work 24/7 for a month."

"Then I underestimated you," Daniel said. "And I underestimated the stakes."

"I'm not sure I follow. And by the way, if you're thinking about going to the police with this—"

Daniel waved away the warning. "I told you, I don't care what you do here. But you are playing a dangerous game. Like they say here in Vegas, all the chips are on the table now, and somebody's about to go all in."

Daniel gave her a look as if to ask, "*Do we understand each other now?*"

The owner nodded. "Okay, what do you need me to do?" she asked.

"I need you to tell me everything. Start with the most recent targets and go back to before you hired Veronica."

The owner of The Frisky Filly held confidentiality as one of her most prized possessions. For some reason, despite the years of building walls, for the first time she felt vulnerable.... Not because of the man walking next to her, but because of the deadly implications his presence seemed to invoke.

CHAPTER THIRTY-SIX

The telephone conversation was more urgent this time.

"He went back to the place. Why?"

"I don't know."

"But I don't understand why he would go back there."

"It doesn't matter. We need to set things up. Stop toying with him, and just get it done."

"But we were having so much fun."

"Maybe that doctor in St. Lucia was right. Maybe you *do* need to get your head checked out."

"Now you've crossed a line. You know how I feel about that."

"I know, and I'm sorry. I'm just on edge. It's time to finish things."

"Okay. Just the way we discussed, right?"

"Just the way we discussed."

CHAPTER THIRTY-SEVEN

"Well, Tom, everything checks out. You'll need to take it easy for a couple of weeks. Make sure you keep taking your pain meds, but in my expert opinion, I'd say you're going to make a full recovery."

"Oh, thank you so much, Doctor," Tom's father said, still feeling like he had to answer for his son.

"Don't thank me," the doctor said, shaking their hands. "I'm just the lucky lout that gets to come in here and give you the good news. Make sure you say thanks to the rest of the staff, especially the nurses. They're the ones who do all the hard work around here. Me, well, they just pay me to look official." He tugged at his lapel like he was trying to look extra sharp. "Oh, and Tom, I'll be in touch about that property. I'm serious about what I said. Three kids, two dogs, and a wife who loves the outdoors don't mix well with a high-rise condo."

"You got it, Doc," Tom said, smiling. He genuinely liked this doctor. He'd gone out of his way to be courteous. Tom had observed how deferential the forty-something physician was to the hospital staff. It wasn't unlike the good officers he'd served under in the Army.

The doctor waved goodbye and left the room.

"You heard what he said, son. You've got to take it easy for a little while. How about a vacation? We could pop over to the coast and soak up some rays, you know, like in the old days when Mom used to drag us all to Disneyland."

"Hey, you said you liked going to Disneyland."

His father smiled. "There's only so many times I can take *It's a Small World*. You loved that damn ride, don't you remember?"

"Of course I do. I still love it. But, Dad, I can't go with you. Not yet."

His father's eyebrows furrowed. "It's that guy, isn't it? Briggs."

"I told you. He's a good guy, Dad, and he needs my help."

"Tom, you're in no condition to help anyone. Have you looked in the mirror?"

"I've been worse," he said. And it was true – the first time he'd come back from Afghanistan, he'd spent two months in the hospital. During that time, barely an hour went by that his father wasn't at his side. They'd become best friends during that time—playing cards, talking, and getting to know one another. Now that it was just the two of them, they recognized Tom's battlefield wounds had been a blessing in disguise. It had given them time to mend their bond, and now they were more best friends than father and son.

"I just can't take the thought of losing you again," his father said, tears welling up in his eyes.

"Dad, this is the way you raised me. I have to help him."

As if on cue, Daniel walked in the door and said, "My ears were ringing down the hall. I hope you weren't talking about me, Tom."

Tom's father looked up in what could have been annoyance, but he quickly played it off. "Hello again, Daniel."

Daniel shook his hand. "How's the patient feeling?"

"Sore as hell," Tom said, easing himself to his feet.

"Well, you *did* slam into a brick wall."

"Well, I don't know about you Marines, but they make us soldiers a lot tougher than a stupid brick wall."

"I don't know how you two can laugh about that," Tom's father said.

"It's part of our DNA, Dad. Helps us deal with the latrine burning detail and the midnight hikes through enemy territory."

His father shook his head. "I'll let you two talk. I'm going to go grab one more coffee and go fetch the car. I'll meet you out front. "

When he had left, Tom struggled to get into his shirt. His body was a patchwork of bruises and cuts. "I was thinking about hitting the clubs tonight topless. What do you think? You think the ladies would go for it?" he said, motioning to his mangled body.

"I think you should leave town," Daniel said, "Just for a couple of days, until things blow over."

"That's funny. My dad just suggested we go to the beach." But there was no humor in his tone. "I'm not leaving, Daniel. You need my help, and so do Jay and Benji."

"It's me they want," Daniel said firmly.

"So, you figured out it's a 'they.'" Tom winced as he slid his feet into his flip-flops.

"It's a 'they.' Has to be."

"And do the cops know?"

"We've sort of come to an agreement," Daniel said.

Tom snorted. "I'm surprised you're even here. Las Vegas PD sent somebody by to ask about you. They had a lot of questions about your past—your time in the military. I didn't have anything to tell them, of course, but I thought you should know."

"Thanks, but all that's settled now."

"It sure didn't seem settled."

"They won't be bothering you anymore," Daniel said confidently. "But you have to promise me that you'll stay out of it. You've already risked enough. I can handle it from here."

"Said the man going out on patrol without the rest of his platoon. Look, Daniel, I don't know what you did before, and I don't really care. You're a good person. The world needs more people like you, so let me help you."

"I want you to understand how much I appreciate that," Daniel said. "I won't forget it. I promise."

"That sounds like a goodbye."

Daniel grinned. "It's not a goodbye. I've just, well—I have a newfound gratitude for the good things in life. I wasn't very good at saying 'thank you' before, but I'm trying."

Tom cocked his head. "What happened to you, anyway? You're not the same guy I met a few days ago."

Daniel shrugged. "I'm not really sure."

"Well, I like the new you, Daniel Briggs. Maybe sometime you'll tell me the secret."

Daniel nodded, but it was obvious that he wasn't going to tell Tom in that hospital room, and that was fine with Tom.

"Okay, I'll stay out of the way. I think I've earned a vacation. But I'm not going to the coast. A nice room at the Bellagio sounds good to me. Does that meet with your approval?"

"You should be fine there. Just see if they'll let you check you in under an alias. And Tom? Please let me handle this. It'll all be over soon."

Tom nodded because he didn't want to speak words of untruth to his friend.

CHAPTER THIRTY-EIGHT

"Hey, Lieutenant, he just left the hospital and hopped in a cab. Do you want me to keep following him?"

"Of course I want you to keep following him."

"Well sir, don't forget that—"

"I know, I know. You're supposed to be off in fifteen minutes. Just let dispatch know where you are, and we'll send your relief out as soon as we can."

The officer exhaled and answered, "Roger." Then he watched as the taxi cab pulled away from the hospital. He was ready to be done with tailing Briggs back and forth. Who was this Briggs guy anyway? Well, it would all be over soon. The officer yawned and he thought how nice it would be to have a real meal. He craved food that didn't come in a Styrofoam container or a paper bag. But as he followed the cab for five minutes, and then another ten he groaned. He wouldn't be enjoying dinner with the dancer from Cirque du Soleil. "Lieutenant, he's headed back out of town again."

"Same way as before?"

"So far but—wait—they just turned. They're not headed

towards The Frisky Filly." It was dark and the officer had a hard time getting his bearings. "I'll let you know if they stop."

"Don't lose them," Salazar said.

"Who do you think I am, a rookie?" the officer said, but the transmit button wasn't depressed. He drove on into the night until finally he saw the brake lights of the cab up ahead. They were literally in the middle of nowhere. There were still cars streaming by. It would be impossible for him not to look totally obvious if he pulled over to the side of the road. So, he kept going and passed the cab. He saw Briggs get out of the taxi and start walking away.

"Where the hell is he going?" He grabbed the radio and called it in. "Lieutenant, the cab just let him out in the middle of the desert." The officer could imagine the obscenities spewing from Salazar's mouth.

"Talk to the cab driver. Arrest him if you have to."

"But I already passed him."

"Then make a U-turn!"

"Roger," was all the officer could say even though he wanted to curse back. Thankfully, the cab hadn't moved by the time he'd completed his U-turn. In fact, it looked like the driver was just waiting for him. *Careful now*, the officer told himself. A dark road one-on-one encounter was an ex-con's wet dream. This particular officer had had more than one close call on nighttime traffic stops. He was careful, easing out of the vehicle, hand resting on his weapon. He waved at the driver. The cabbie waved back.

"Please get out of the car," the officer said. He was maybe a car length away.

"Oh, yeah. Sure. Sure," the driver replied, stepping out slowly, hands raised. "No problems here, Officer. Just doing my duty for the community."

This should be fun, the officer thought. He immediately

pegged the driver as one of those cartoon caricatures—the kind that never shut up.

"He said you were following us, but that was pretty quick," the driver said.

It took a moment for the officer to realize the man was talking about Briggs. "What else did he say to you?"

"He didn't say much. He just told me to keep driving, and then when we got here he told me to stop. Gave me a couple hundred bucks, though, so that's cool. Hey, is he in some kind of trouble?"

The officer frowned. The driver posed no threat. "Do you make it a habit of driving strangers out to the middle of nowhere?"

The driver shrugged, oblivious to any danger. "I do my job, man. You want to go somewhere? I drive you. The pickups I really hate are the sorority girls. You know, the ones that are all boozed up and throw up in the back of my cab? That's a real pain in the ass. But hell, easy money like this? I wish I could do that every day."

"Do you mind if I look in the cab?" the officer asked.

"Be my guest. He didn't leave anything. I already checked; I always check."

The officer bet he did. It was so easy to pawn a dropped phone or gather a little loose change. It was one of the perks of being in the taxi business.

When his cursory examination was complete, the officer relaxed. "Was he carrying anything?"

"Just a paper bag. Had a couple water bottles in it. Kept sipping from one. Nice enough guy, quiet though. Did I already say that? He had intense eyes. Not like in a mean way. But you know, when you've been driving as long as I have, eyes are pretty much all you see in the rear-view mirror. So, I look at the eyes. Hey, do you mind if I go now? That's dispatch calling, and tonight's a pretty busy night in town."

"Sure. Let me just get your name and license number in case we have any more questions," the officer said.

"Oh, no problem," the cab driver said happily, as if he loved coming down to the police station to chat.

The cab driver was behind the wheel with the engine started when he looked back up at the officer and asked, "Hey did they ever find the person who killed that cop?"

"No, not yet," the officer said.

The cab driver nodded sadly and drove off. The officer tried to figure out how he would tell Lieutenant Salazar that he just lost his target.

CHAPTER THIRTY-NINE

The rookie cop assigned to Pacific Palisades was used to getting these tasks. He was the low man on the totem pole. That meant frisking drunks, searching abandoned warehouses, and helping kids with lost cats. Oh, and investigating empty houses, like he was currently doing. He had heard the stories of loved ones calling from far away reporting, "Grandpa Joe won't pick up his phone," or "We haven't heard from Aunt Betty in three weeks." Officer Ted Franklin wondered, naively, how many of those calls happened just because the "disappeared" family member didn't want to talk to the family.

It was an extremely safe neighborhood. Sure, there were the occasional break-ins. Home invasions were rare, and murders were rarer still. Driving to the house, the officer possessed an inch of confidence in the report and a healthy splash of boredom poured on top. He pulled into the driveway of the impressive Colonial-style home.

"Dispatch, this is Officer Franklin. I've just arrived at 235 Milton. Please acknowledge."

"Roger that, Franklin. Don't go inventing electricity all by yourself."

Franklin ignored the comment. Their gibes no longer bothered him. His last name had instantly given him the moniker "Benjamin Franklin."

He sighed. Franklin could have applied for a downtown LAPD assignment. Or he could have moved to San Diego. But he'd requested to work in Pacific Palisades because he thought it would be interesting. And, to be honest, his girlfriend liked the area, so that was a plus.

Up until now, he'd done everything except mop the floors. Franklin understood it was just part of being the new guy. But it had been seven months, and he was more than ready to move up the ranks. *Just maybe a newbie would start soon.*

Officer Franklin was mindful to lock the car when he exited. He wouldn't want any rich kids trying to steal his car. That would give the boys at the station a new water cooler topic, at his expense.

He walked to the door of the residence, just like he'd been trained, always ready to grab his holstered weapon. The porch light was off, and he congratulated himself for being smart enough to bring his flashlight.

He knocked on the door. No answer. He reached over and rang the doorbell twice. Still, no answer. He was about to call it a night and just write it up as "no one at home." Then he thought, *Why not just try the doorknob?*

The doorknob turned. *Maybe the deadbolt's set.* But it wasn't. The door, unlatched, opened with ease. Before switching on his flashlight, Officer Franklin staggered back, hit in the face by a wave of putrescence.

He retched once and then again. The nausea, in repetitive waves, washed over him. Once he was positive there was nothing left in his stomach to vomit, Franklin stood up like a colt standing for the first time – unsure and a bit wobbly.

Staggering to the police cruiser, Franklin began taking long, deep breaths. Smelling his own breath, he fished through his pockets for a breath mint which he deposited quickly into his mouth. When he was confident he could speak clearly, he unlocked the car, grabbing the police radio.

"Requesting immediate backup at 235 Milton Drive. I repeat, I need backup at 235 Milton. I repeat, immediate backup required at 235 Milton Drive."

Dispatch's voice sounded quite serious now. "Roger. Officer Franklin found the Easter Bunny."

Franklin could have sworn he heard giggling in the background. *Assholes.*

Once more he radioed in to dispatch. He repeated his request with more insistence. But this time he had remembered to use the code signifying he'd found a dead body. Franklin also asked for an ambulance to be dispatched.

"Roger that," came the curt reply. The peals of laughter were gone.

A moment later, a nearby officer reported he was on his way to the scene.

Thank God, Franklin thought. Thank God he hadn't puked in front of his peers.

———

MARGARET TAYLOR WAS aware there were still words being spoken, but she was unable to respond. She knew there were words coming out of the phone, but she couldn't respond. She'd arrived at the hotel minutes before in sore need of a hot bath and a drink. *How could he be dead?* she thought. She'd left so many messages on his phone. *How could he be dead?*

"Ma'am, are you still there?" the officer asked.

"Yes, I'm sorry."

"We're still processing the scene, ma'am. We'll call you as soon as we know more."

"Was his death due to natural causes, or was it something else?"

"I don't mean to upset you, but there may have been foul play involved. Do you know of anyone who would want to harm your ex-husband?"

"What? No. I don't think so, but I haven't seen him in quite some time," Margaret Taylor said. In her heart, she knew—maybe she'd always known. The fact that the revelation had always been there, the seed deposited years before, intensified her grief tenfold.

Without another word, she hung up the phone and walked to the mini-bar.

CHAPTER FORTY

The phone call connected with a garbled squelch.

"He's headed into the desert."

"What are you going to do?"

"I'm going in after him."

"Okay, just be careful."

"I always am; besides, he's unarmed."

"Okay, but are you still sure you want to end it this way?"

"Yes, it's time to move on. Besides, I'm bored. I'm ready for a vacation."

"All right then, but be careful."

"You *already* said that."

"I know. It's just that—"

"Don't tell me you're worried."

"*I am* the one that worries."

"Well, don't. This is an easy one."

"You said the same thing about Saint Lucia."

"That was totally different, but you're right. I'll be careful."

"Okay. I'll see you soon."

CHAPTER FORTY-ONE

I t was an unusually mild night for this time of year. The temperature hovered in the high seventies. The moon was full, and it illuminated the traveler's measured steps. Daniel knew he was being followed, but that's what he wanted.

It was such a strange sensation. He'd been aware of his gifts before, but now it felt like somebody had ratcheted up the power. It was like every nerve ending in his body and every brain wave were now heightened. It did nothing to deaden the pain of loss, but it allowed him to look at it from a different angle. The Stranger was no longer a stranger. He and The Beast walked next to him, even though Daniel couldn't see them.

There were still so many questions to be asked, and so many answers left to be excavated. Whereas before he might have worried about such a thing, now he had absolute confidence that they would come. It was strange. Now that he was no longer thinking of himself, but of others, he felt like he could let go of the worry. It wasn't completely gone. The transformation was not yet complete. But he had faith that it would take him over, body and soul. The thought made him smile.

Lose oneself in giving, came the voice, soft and sweet, as if it had been blown in on the summer breeze. Yes, it was like playing by a new playbook. The tactics and strategy were similar, yet there were subtle differences. It was like the difference between having a friend vs. having a brother. One was like ankle deep water—refreshing for a time—made to feel permanent. The other was chest deep—all in—you couldn't change it.

That's what he felt now as he walked—free for the first time in years. He could almost feel the crosshairs on the back of his head, but he wasn't worried. He was confident, not in a cocky way, but in a way that felt good. He felt that his life was finally meant for something. It was meant for many things, and at that particular moment, it was not meant for dying.

DANIEL INHALED THE DESERT AIR, letting it fill him, propelling him forward. Yes, he felt the enemy coming, but he also felt his friend, and without turning to regard him, the voice whispered, *I am here. You are not alone.*

———

THE ASSASSIN PICKED a careful path across the desert floor. Silent steps borne of endless practice. The Marine sniper was well ahead of the assassin now, but the natural killer wasn't concerned. They were walking through miles of open desert, and it was nearly impossible to find a place to hide. Briggs was illuminated by the moon, whereas the assassin was shielded by the orb's position behind them. Yes, it was a perfect night to stalk—a perfect night to kill. The cat and mouse game would soon be complete, and then they would move on to other things. They always moved on to other things.

To kill for fun, thought the assassin, and then the assassin's other half's warning sounded subconsciously. Yes, it was better to do it from far away. But the assassin wanted to be closer. All that was needed was to skirt to the side to find a better vantage point.

There it was up ahead. A hill. Briggs's stride was taking him straight for it. The assassin considered the options, and the hill zeroed in as the perfect chance. Briggs would pass through, leaving a perfect lane for the killer to take a shot.

No need to hurry. They had all night. The assassin could keep this up for days, with a rifle cradled in confident arms, and a pack full of provisions carried on a body honed from years of toil and practice. The assassin was the *perfect* weapon.

Eyes flickered from the target to the ground, back and forth, selecting the perfect path. Silent and careful—always careful. The eyes flickered up, back to the Marine sniper, who had been the perfect stroke of luck.

Wait. Where did he go? One second Briggs had been there, and then he'd disappeared. Impossible. The assassin scanned left and right carefully. Nothing. *No way*. There was nowhere to hide.

The assassin looked at the base of the hill, weapon at the ready, calculating the distance since Briggs had last been seen. *Impossible. He was right here*, the assassin thought, and then the truth became known. There it was. It would have been almost undetectable, even in broad daylight. A small drop off led to an old riverbed that snaked along the same path. Briggs must have taken the slight detour, and sure enough, there was his form, weaving his way toward the hill in the slithering depression.

The assassin breathed in relief, confident once again, as the killer slipped into the ancient riverbed. The shot could have been taken here, but the assassin wanted something better. The perfect shot was the best way to end it.

Onward they went until Briggs reached the base of the hill and started climbing. He never once looked back. Then the assassin realized where Briggs was going. It hadn't been obvious in the dead of night, but now a map of the area coalesced in the assassin's mind, and there it was. The ranch from the coyote hunt. The one Tom's friends had told them about during their bloody interrogation.

Yes, that had to be it. Briggs was going to see the old rancher. The assassin had considered that option before, but Briggs had already made another trip to the ranch. Now he was once again taking a late-night stroll across the desert. It might have seemed strange to a normal human being, but the assassin was used to seeing strange things.

After some quick mental math, the assassin figured at their current leisurely pace, it was maybe another hour on foot until they got to the ranch. He wouldn't get that far. The plan was to leave Briggs's body in the desert. Maybe someone would find him, and maybe they wouldn't. That didn't really matter. The key was the challenge. It was time to make a move now, so the assassin cut right, careful not to dislodge anything that might give the position away. Time to maneuver around and cut him off. Time to end the game and claim the prize.

The spot the assassin picked was perfect. It was just on the other side of the hill's crest. The path Briggs was on would take him there directly. It was as if nature tailor-made the ambush point just for this moment. A tight funnel bordered by the steep rise of the hill to its peak on one side, and a cutaway cliff on the other. It was like God had taken a knife and sliced the back side of the hill clean off. It was the exact point the killer needed. The assassin moved beyond it to monitor Briggs's progress.

Crouched within an indentation to avoid detection, every few seconds the assassin would chance a look. Briggs's form was moving up the hill now. *Faster*, the assassin thought. *Have to move quickly now. Maybe something close in would be best.* Briggs was completely unaware; it could be perfect. The assassin never told her other half this, but it was better to see the life drain from a target's eyes. It was better to feel that last hot breath as they drifted into nothingness. Yes, that was how the assassin would do it. Close in until the life force could be sucked from the target.

The assassin went back to the ambush point, hidden from view. The only downside was that Briggs couldn't be seen now. But the assassin was confident in the sniper's path. The other half wouldn't be happy. There was still time. The assassin stopped, pulled out the phone, shielding the dim light and sent a text.

Headed to the ranch. Meet me there, and then pressed send. The reply was almost instantaneous. It was how they worked. Always monitoring the phone. The reply was a simple *okay*.

Plans were now coordinated. The assassin waited impatiently, already tasting the blood that was soon to come. Maybe they would kill the rancher too. Maybe they would just have some fun with him. It didn't matter. They would do it together like they always did. Two as one.

CHAPTER FORTY-TWO

The assassin didn't have time to enjoy the view. It was reassuring to see their calculations had been precise. From off in the distance, the assassin could see the lights of the ranch. Once again, the assassin marveled at the ambush point. Not only was it perfect for the kill shot, but it also offered an amazing view of the valley beyond. With the moon casting its glow upon the Earth, the assassin thought it was a fitting spot for the night's errand.

The assassin waited and listened. Two minutes went by. Nothing. Maybe Briggs had stopped to take a break and drink some of the water he had purchased at the hospital gift shop. Another three minutes went by and still there was no sign of Daniel Briggs.

The assassin peeked up the trail. He must be coming, but still there was no sign of him. *Patience*. The assassin waited another two minutes, attempting to tamp down the anxiety. Maybe Briggs had turned around or maybe he stopped to take a nap. Maybe—

But then the assassin heard a noise. It sounded like a

handful of pebbles rolling downhill. He was coming, and he was nearby.

The assassin considered grabbing the rifle again but settled for the knife. The blade was sharp and compact. It was the perfect weapon for stabbing into a neck or slicing across a man's eyes. The assassin liked the neck; it put on a bloody good show.

The assassin counted down the seconds. It was imperative to time the strike perfectly. The appointed time came when the assassin knew Briggs would be within striking range, yet he still wasn't there. The nervous energy made the assassin take another look up the trail to where he should be by now. Suddenly, a shadow materialized overhead. The assassin rolled over to face the falling form, trying to get the blade in position. But the shadow knocked the weapon away, falling heavily on top of the assassin. The air blasted from lungs already constricted, ready for the attack. The assassin tried to roll away but was pinned down by strong hands and legs.

A familiar itch of panic rose in the assassin's throat. The rifle was too far away, and the knife had fallen over the edge. Briggs's surprise was complete. It had been perfectly executed, something the assassin should have done. The roles should have been reversed.

And then the pressure let up.

"Get to your feet," Briggs said.

Veronica Taylor stood up, ignoring the pain in her knee and hip from where she had fallen. Daniel stepped back and covered her path to the rifle.

"You don't look surprised to see me," Veronica said, trying to sound nonchalant. In fact, she was trying to figure out a way she could still kill Briggs.

Daniel didn't say a word; he just stared at her. She expected some kind of babbling questions about the child or maybe the others, but none came. It put her off kilter. That was a feeling she had never liked.

Maybe her other half was right. Maybe she did need to see someone. She couldn't help the words from coming out, "When did you figure it out?"

Daniel still didn't move. He had changed. They had both seen it. It was an interesting transformation that made their hunt that much more appealing. It was like a fine wine aged to perfection and ready for ingestion.

Veronica grabbed onto an idea.

"Your rancher friend is going to die."

Now there was a flicker of concern on Daniel's face.

"How did you know I was going to be there?" Daniel asked.

"Oh, we figured it out," Veronica said, stretching her neck from side to side to loosen the tension.

"Who is *we*?"

Veronica paused until she was sure that he wasn't kidding. Then she laughed. *Oh, he hasn't figured it all out. Oh, that makes this so much more fun.*

"Who is it, Veronica? *Who's* helping you?"

"You think I'm going to tell you?" Veronica pointed at Daniel. "You should see the look on your face. You had me fooled. I really thought when you weren't surprised to see me a second ago; you had figured it out. But you haven't. You're too late." Veronica pointed back over her shoulder to where the ranch lay. "He's going to die because of you—just like the others. How will you live with that knowledge?"

"Live with what?" Daniel asked.

"All that death. I mean—I know how I deal with it. I've never had a problem with it. Call it something in my DNA. Even as a kid I didn't care. But you—you did it for a living. You killed people, and you watched your friends die. I don't know how you can live with yourself. Maybe I should go buy you another bottle of Jack Daniels. How long do you think it will take to find the answer in there?"

Daniel didn't budge. Veronica was hoping that he would come forward—that he would try to hit or grab her. She had read his file. It was amazing what a few phone calls could dig up. The poor Marine was a broken hero.

"Tell me Daniel, how heavy does Nathaniel's death weigh on your conscience?"

"That wasn't my fault," Daniel said.

The peals of laughter came straight from Veronica's belly. "Oh, is that what you think? You mean, *that* wasn't your fault? Let me tell you something, hero, his death *was* your fault. You see, *we* did the math. We knew you were tough; we knew that you could take the physical pain. But a little boy? We saw how you connected with him. We saw that you wanted to help him. So, what's the best way to put a hero on his ass? Take away the thing that he wants most."

Daniel took a step towards her.

Yes, come closer, Veronica thought.

"You're a monster," Daniel said.

"And you sound like the naive hero you are. You aren't ready for this. You'll never be ready for this. You think you know who I am? You have no idea. I kill for the sheer fun of it. I enjoy it. I dream about it, and I taste it with every meal. What do you say we finish this the old-fashioned way? Hand-to-hand combat—Mano a mano—Or me and mano?" Veronica tempted.

She sensed that he was trying to take another step forward. That's when she would make her move. No one ever expected a woman of her size to be their equal. She had been well trained. She had been put through the ringer and came out like a hardened steel rod. She could crush stone with her hands. It would only be a matter of moments before she did the same to Briggs's head.

"No," Daniel said, without stepping forward. In fact, he stepped back and grabbed the rifle.

"Come on, I'm just a little girl," Veronica teased. "You don't need that thing."

"I'm not going to shoot you," he said. "I'm taking you back to town."

"I'm not going back."

"You don't have a choice."

"There's always a choice, Daniel. Just like you had a choice of whether to talk to Nathaniel. You chose to insert yourself into our lives."

Veronica was willing to die. But she wanted the time and place to be of her choosing.

"Put the gun down, Daniel. I promise to *not* take it easy on you."

The rifle's barrel rose until it was pointed straight at her chest.

"We're leaving *now*."

Just then, in the distance Veronica saw headlights. Daniel must have seen them too because he urgently said, "Veronica, turn around and start walking down the path."

She looked at him, the poor damaged hero. He was trying to save the day once again. Little did he know he would be too late. He was trying to do the right thing. While it might be seen as noble to most people, Veronica viewed it as pure weakness. She had spent her life perfecting the art of strength and never, ever showing weakness. It started out as an act, but it now defined her very being.

All those tests had brought her here to this moment.

"I wish I could be around to see the new you," Veronica said. "Oh, and to see the look on your face when more of your friends die. But I have to go now."

"You're not going anywhere," Daniel said.

"I stopped taking orders from men a long time ago. I'm not going to start again now."

She locked eyes with him for a long moment. Then she gave him a quick two-finger salute, pivoted, and executed a perfect swan dive over the cliff face.

CHAPTER FORTY-THREE

Daniel ran like he'd never run before. He'd watched Veronica plunge into the darkness, and he could just make out the shape of her body splattered on the desert floor. At that point, he hit the trail, sprinting to the property in the distance. Running all out, he arrived at his destination in fifteen minutes. He recognized the white Cadillac parked out front.

Only after his breathing had slowed and he had checked the rifle over a last time did he enter the house. He was aware he might be too late to save the rancher's life.

The property was eerily quiet, like it had been abandoned for forty years, except for the lingering smells of dinner. There was a light on in the kitchen. It acted like a brilliant magnet pulling him into the house. When he entered, he imagined the rancher slumped in a chair and tied down. That is unless Veronica's accomplice had already killed him. He peeked inside the kitchen which he found empty.

Then he recognized his mistake; he'd gone in too quickly. In validation of his concern, a familiar voice asked, "Are you looking for me?" Daniel froze. There was no way beyond black magic. *Was this one final test?* How could he have gotten it so wrong?

He had thought maybe it was the owner of The Frisky Filly; she had been *much* too accommodating. Or maybe it was one of the police officers—Salazar?

But he was wrong on both counts. He turned to face the person. As the living room light flickered on, he stood staring in disbelief at the woman who had just executed the perfect suicide drop off the side of a cliff.

"Veronica?"

She had a shotgun leveled at him, motioning for him to drop the rifle. He did as she ordered, setting it down slowly, careful not to make any sudden moves.

"Where is my sister?" she asked. Like the first mechanism that clicks in the first of a series of dueling cogs and spinning contraptions, his mind finally caught hold.

"You're twins," Daniel said.

"I asked you—where is my sister?"

There was no shakiness in the woman's voice, and her body was tense yet relaxed, just the way his would have been in this type of situation.

Daniel artfully dodged the question. "Your father's dead, isn't he?"

"He was never *our* father," she snapped.

"He was good to both you and Nathaniel."

"You don't know anything about our lives."

Then the realization hit. "Oh! He found out about you two, didn't he?" The narrowing in Veronica's eyes was the only affirmation he received. "At least tell me how you pulled this off. Did he know you came as a package deal?"

"Of course not."

"Let me guess. You took turns playing daughter, while the other one was somewhere else?" He received no answer, not that Daniel needed one. All the pieces finally fit into place, explaining the lapses and the impossibility of Veronica being in two places at once. It really had been an ingenious and deadly plan. "Last question—I promise—and then you're free to do whatever you want. Was Nathaniel yours?"

Now he got the first hint she was not void of emotion. Veronica's knuckles went white. "Where is my sister?"

Daniel wasn't going to be the one to tell her. She would have to figure that out on her own. Besides, he couldn't shake the feeling that his entire existence had solidified into this very moment. He had endured incredible things with his body, and he probably could have done something sensational to deliver the death blow. Previously, that's exactly what he would have done. But now, as he stared at Veronica, he just wanted to understand. His newfound curiosity and acceptance of both life and death wanted to mine the intricacies of this woman's mind.

"Why did you kill Nathaniel?"

Veronica didn't answer. She had the hard stance of a guard waiting for a commander to walk through the door.

"She made you kill him, didn't she?"

"It was the only way," she said, as if trying to convince herself one last time.

"You're a mother, and you were forced to kill your child. I'm sorry, Veronica. No one should have to do that."

The shotgun slipped down an inch.

"I loved him."

"I know you did."

"But he saw us together, just like my stepfather had." She stomped her foot like an impetuous child. "We tried to play it off, but Nathaniel wouldn't let it go."

"She had to keep your secret, but *she* also made you do the dirty work," Daniel guessed.

"No, we made the decision together. I don't know why

I'm telling you this." Her eyes refocused. "Where is she? If you hurt her—"

"I promise you, I did not hurt her."

"Then tell me where she is."

"I'm sorry for your loss."

Veronica's eyes went wide. "What are you saying?"

"I'm telling you that your sister is dead."

"You hurt her?"

"I did no such thing."

Veronica was shaking now, "She was the only person I had. She was the only one that understood. We took care of each other."

"Then let me take care of you," Daniel said. "It won't be easy, but I promise I'll help you."

Strangely, despite her despicable act, Daniel believed every word he spoke. The woman standing in front of him was a killer, but something had happened to make her a killer. Maybe it was out of necessity, or maybe she had just followed her sister's whims. For some reason, in that moment, Daniel felt empathy toward her and the situation where she now found herself.

"I don't believe you. I didn't feel anything." Veronica said, as if when her sister died some alarm in her soul would have been triggered.

"She's dead," Daniel said.

For the first time, Veronica's eyes left Daniel's. They flitted back and forth, as if she was searching for something. She was murmuring, talking to herself, babbling really. "She said it was done. She said it would be easy. Yes. That's what she said. That's it, yes." Then she looked back at Daniel, her confidence renewed.

"Tell me where you left her body."

"I can show you," Daniel said.

She motioned with the shotgun to the door.

Daniel had no doubt that if he tried to run, she would take him down with a single shot. Veronica #2 was no longer unglued. She was steadily becoming focused, and the Marine sniper held no illusions about how this would end. At least he felt the consolation that when he walked out the front door, he would not do so alone. The Beast was strangely quiet but present, and he knew the stranger was walking next to him.

Whatever comes, will come, Daniel thought to himself, feeling oddly at peace with the situation.

Daniel pointed into the desert, the way he had come.

"If you head straight for that hill, your sister is at the base of it, on this side." He turned to face her. She still had her weapon pointed at him. Her eyes squinted toward her sister's resting spot. Then her eyes refocused on him.

"I bet you feel stupid now for helping me at that bus station. You could have avoided all of this, you know. That's always how these things start. Someone thinks they can help, and then we suck them right in. It's so easy to do, especially with men."

"I will never regret trying to help you," Daniel said. "And I don't regret the brief time I spent with Nathaniel. Forever, I'll remember him." Then Daniel thought of the one thing he'd forgotten to ask. "Where's the old man who lives here?"

"He wasn't here."

That's strange, Daniel thought. The old man's truck was still on the property. *At least he was safe.*

Daniel waited patiently. He didn't know why Veronica didn't shoot. Maybe she was accustomed to getting orders from her sister. Maybe she didn't want to admit it was over. If she killed Daniel, she would have to gather her sister's body, and then she would truly be alone. Daniel knew how it felt to be alone, wandering aimlessly through life with every turn tighter than the one before.

He made a decision that his last words would be words of kindness, not of hatred.

"Thank you for letting me spend time with Nathaniel. He was a great kid, and I'm sure he's looking down on us right now, hoping that you'll do the right thing."

The shaking and emotion from her he'd seen in the house did not make a second appearance. Instead, her lips paled in the moonlight, and she took a step closer to him.

"Do not say his name *ever* again. My son is dead."

Daniel put his hands in the air. "If you're going to shoot me, do it now. I'm sure the police have figured out where I've gone and they'll be here soon. Just get it over with. I *promise* I won't move. "

Veronica's finger tightened on the trigger.

So, this was it—the final showdown. And yet, Daniel did not feel afraid. He was confident in his actions of the day. He knew he'd done the right thing. He could live or die in peace. *Peace*. That small word had left an indelible mark on his soul.

"Shoot," he said again.

Veronica leaned in just perceptibly, poised to end it all.

Daniel closed his eyes, and he said a prayer.

CHAPTER FORTY-FOUR

The gunshot thundered and Daniel didn't move, surprised to not feel pain. Maybe he'd already gone. Maybe it was that fast. Life snatched by the reaper in the blink of an eye.

Then he opened his eyes at the sound of another gunshot and he saw that Veronica was no longer in front of him. In fact, she'd been thrown a good five feet to his right. Her arm was still moving, trying to push her body up when the third shot hit her square in the side of the face. The movement stopped.

Where did the shots come from? A large caliber weapon. Maybe a .30-06. It had the effect of sounding like a cannon at close range. Daniel turned to see where the shots had come from and then there they were: the old rancher, Tom and his father and even the owner of The Frisky Filly. They rushed out as one. An M1 Garand was cradled like a baby in the rancher's arms.

"Daniel, are you okay?" Tom asked.

"Yeah, I'm fine. You guys sure know how to make an entrance."

"I'm sorry it took us so long. Abraham called us and luckily we were on the way."

"How did you know I was here?"

"Lieutenant Salazar called me," the owner of The Frisky Filly said. "He asked why you might be coming out this far in the desert, and I said I didn't know. I put two and two together and I figured you were coming out to Abraham's place. The next thing I did was call Tom."

"Abraham—your name is Abraham," Daniel said to the old rancher.

"The name my mother gave me."

Daniel stuck out his hand, "It's a pleasure to meet you, Abraham. I apologize for never asking your name before."

"It never came up so I never thought to offer it myself, but apology accepted, Daniel Briggs."

The five of them just stood there for a long, long moment. Each digested what had happened both in the preceding minutes and in the preceding days. As Daniel stood there, he couldn't help but think that these people, these friends who he'd met not long before, had made the rash decision to come to his aid. His aid. A stranger. What was he but a stranger to them? And yet—

Daniel marveled at this, and that when he'd cast down his weapon, relinquishing the warrior inside and taming the frightening Beast who had allowed him to do so many vengeful deeds, that this had finally opened up the space for something else. Trust? Trust in his friends. Trust in the world that things would come out the way they should—or maybe it was just faith. Yes, that was it. Faith in all things.

"What are we going to do about that body?" Tom's father asked. And then, as if to accentuate the point, the first wails of sirens sounded in the distance followed by the flashing lights of a line of police cars coming down the single lane road.

"You all saw what happened. I'll take the fall if I need to," Abraham said without hesitation.

"It won't come to that," Daniel said reaching into his pocket. He held up a black object for the others to see.

"What's that?" Tom's father asked.

"It's a digital recorder. I *may* have swiped it from the doctor at the hospital. It's got everything."

"But how could you know?" Tom asked.

Daniel shrugged. "Something told me to grab it, so I did."

They all shared a relieved laugh as the caravan of police cars pulled onto the property. It was a night none of them would ever forget, least of all Daniel.

EPILOGUE

The next few days were a swirl of emotions and endless activity. Once the police arrived at Abraham's property, they searched the stolen Cadillac, revealing the plastic-wrapped bodies of Jay and Benji. Lieutenant Salazar was ready to pin the murders on Daniel. Luckily, the sniper produced the digital recorder that contained his conversation with both Veronicas. After that, it just took some good old-fashioned police legwork to confirm the story of the twins.

Margaret Taylor was found stumbling drunk in her hotel room. After sobering up, she told the police that Veronica had been adopted at the age of nine. It was supposed to be a package deal. During that time, Veronica's sister, Violet, was dealing with multiple run-ins with both the law and the orphanage's staff. Margaret and her then husband made the painful decision to not adopt Violet. They had, of course, promised to come back if she got her act together. But that never had happened. Veronica's sister disappeared. It was if she had been wiped from the face of the earth, as far as the authorities could determine. It was rare that many resources were allocated to look for an runaway orphan.

Now that both sisters were dead, it could only be assumed they had kept in touch. At some point, it was suspected, they'd made a pact to stick together. When examined side-by-side at the morgue, it was uncanny how similar they looked. The coroner confirmed both women had undergone multiple identical plastic surgeries to ensure they'd pass as carbon copies of each other.

The scope of the investigation widened. The images of the sisters were circulated, and their movements were tracked all over the world. Their presence was confirmed in Germany, the Middle East, Jamaica, St. Lucia, and even Japan. In their wake, many deaths (mostly men) were attributed to the nomad assassins. Witnesses said they'd only seen one sister at a time. They were unaware twins existed. Veronica was described as a thrill-seeker. She pushed the limits of what her body could achieve and endure. She engaged in activities like weapons training and martial arts, windsurfing and heli-skiing. It was obvious the twins enjoyed living their lives on the razor's edge. Most recently, their adventurous life had led them to Las Vegas. They had attempted to extort The Frisky Filly after learning the owner was selling delicate information on the black market.

The run-in with Daniel had been mere happenstance. When the sisters discovered they might be able to lure a future Medal of Honor recipient into a duel, the temptation must have been too much for the siblings to pass up. The lies piled up, including the story about the cancer and the one about Nathaniel being sick. Two separate physicians confirmed that the opposite was true. No one had been sick, except for maybe the sisters, in their heads.

After completing the questioning and finding what answers could be unearthed, the case was closed. Tom,

Daniel, and Abraham sat around a table at the bar where Tom and Daniel had first met. They each had a shot glass in one hand.

Tom raised his offering, "To Jay and Benji."

Abraham and Daniel raised their shot glasses and clinked together. "To Jay and Benji," they repeated in unison.

Two days earlier, they'd attended a quiet ceremony held in Santa Monica. Everyone was still mourning the loss of Nathaniel. In a spot overlooking the Pacific Ocean, the young boy was laid to rest next to his grandfather. It was a beautiful and fitting way to say goodbye. Now they were saying their final goodbyes to two men who had been friends with Tom for his entire life, although Daniel had barely known them.

Tom downed his drink. Abraham and Daniel refrained from drinking. They set their shot glasses back on the table.

"Well I guess that's it then," Tom said, setting his glass on the table as well. "Daniel, have you considered my offer?"

Tom's offer had been very generous. He and his father wanted Daniel to work at their real estate company. In Tom's own words, Daniel was "a perfect fit." He had also offered Daniel a place to live.

Daniel had had time to think about the offer. He felt truly blessed to have a friend like Tom and a mentor like Abraham. While the investigation was being wrapped up he'd been warned against leaving Las Vegas. Thus, he spent his nights at Abraham's ranch. He helped with the crops and the livestock. The men talked long into the nights, sharing stories from their pasts. During those days and nights, they found they shared a common ground—life. Both had chosen to embrace life wholeheartedly.

"I think I'm going to stick around Vegas for a while," Daniel said. Tom perked up. "But I can't take your offer. I just don't think I'm the right fit for real estate. *You've* got the personality for it, but—"

"Oh, c'mon, you'll do great," Tom assured him.

"Thanks. I really do appreciate it. Please thank your dad for me, but I've got some things to figure out."

Daniel looked at Abraham; he nodded his understanding.

Tom didn't let up. "But you've got to do something for money, right? At least let me bring you in to do some work. Fix up some houses or something," Tom said.

"I'll think about it. In the meantime, I've gotta see what else this city has to offer. Maybe make a few more friends." Daniel smiled at Abraham. One of the recurring themes of their nightly talks had been the devilish curse of the drunk— the man in pain who shunned all friendships. Daniel was coming out of that funk now, and it was Abraham who prodded him into exploring his newfound freedom.

Tom must have seen that Daniel's mind was made up, so he dove into another story instead. He started telling the tale of the developer he was working with. This developer was trying to get land for pennies on the dollar, "But lemme tell you about what he said when I told him to lay off the hookah pipe." Everyone laughed, and when Tom felt he'd roped them in, he went on. Each man, in his own way, enjoyed being in the others' company.

As Tom talked, Daniel's mind drifted to the future. He was done running—of that he was sure. He had no idea what the final masterpiece that was his life would look like. But he had absolute faith that if he spent the rest of his days helping others, at some point, he would be connected with men and women just like him, who sought to do the right thing, no matter the consequences.

What an amazing family to be a part of, he thought. *But when will it happen?*

"Have patience," the voice said. "Enjoy what I have given you, and enjoy what you have chosen to give yourself. I am with you. *Always* I am with you. You are special, Daniel

Briggs. You are one of a kind, made in my likeness. Show the world who *you* are, and then they will know who *I* am."

With that Daniel smiled, thought of the future, and dreamed of what he might find.

———

I hope you enjoyed this story.
If you did, please take a moment to write a review on AMAZON. Even the short ones help!

GET A FREE COPY OF THE CORPS JUSTICE PREQUEL SHORT STORY, *GOD-SPEED*, JUST FOR SUBSCRIBING AT CG-COOPER.COM

ALSO BY C. G. COOPER

The Corps Justice Series In Order (also featuring Daniel Briggs):

Back To War

Council Of Patriots

Prime Asset

Presidential Shift

National Burden

Lethal Misconduct

Moral Imperative

Disavowed

Chain Of Command

Papal Justice

The Zimmer Doctrine

Sabotage

Liberty Down

Sins Of The Father

Corps Justice Short Stories:

Chosen

God-Speed

Running

The Daniel Briggs Novels:

Adrift

Fallen

Broken

Tested

The Tom Greer Novels

A Life Worth Taking

The Spy In Residence Novels

What Lies Hidden

The Alex Knight Novels:

Breakout

The Stars & Spies Series:

Backdrop

The Patriot Protocol Series:

The Patriot Protocol

The Chronicles of Benjamin Dragon:

Benjamin Dragon – Awakening

Benjamin Dragon – Legacy

Benjamin Dragon - Genesis

ABOUT THE AUTHOR

C. G. Cooper is the USA TODAY and AMAZON
BESTSELLING author of the CORPS JUSTICE novels
(including spinoffs), The Chronicles of Benjamin Dragon and
the Patriot Protocol series.

Cooper grew up in a Navy family and traveled from one
Naval base to another as he fed his love of books and a
fledgling desire to write.

Upon graduating from the University of Virginia with a
degree in Foreign Affairs, Cooper was commissioned in the

United States Marine Corps and went on to serve six years as an infantry officer. C. G. Cooper's final Marine duty station was in Nashville, Tennessee, where he fell in love with the laid-back lifestyle of Music City.

His first published novel, BACK TO WAR, came out of a need to link back to his time in the Marine Corps. That novel, written as a side project, spawned many follow-on novels, several exciting spinoffs, and catapulted Cooper's career.

Cooper lives just south of Nashville with his wife, three children, and their German shorthaired pointer, Liberty, who's become a popular character in the Corps Justice novels.

When he's not writing or hosting his podcast, Books In 30, Cooper spends time with his family, does his best to improve his golf handicap, and loves to shed light on the ongoing fight of everyday heroes.

Cooper loves hearing from readers and responds to every email personally.

To connect with C. G. Cooper visit
www.cg-cooper.com

ACKNOWLEDGMENTS

More thanks to my Beta Readers:

Kim, Nancy, Phil, Susan, Glenda, Karen, Marsha, Pam, Melissa, Marry, Ron, Michael, Wanda, Kathryn, CaryLory, Gary, John, Craig, Chip, Anne, Don and Judith. Thank you!

Made in the USA
Monee, IL
20 July 2021

73955546R00132